The Mystery of
Banshee Towers

Also by Enid Blyton in the Mystery series

Enid Blyton

The Mystery of Banshee Towers

Text illustrations by Jenny Chapple

DRAGON
Granada Publishing

Dragon Books
Granada Publishing Ltd
8 Grafton Street, London W1X 3LA

Published by Dragon Books 1969
Reprinted 1971 (twice), 1972, 1973, 1975, 1976,
1977, 1979, 1980, 1983, 1984

First published in Great Britain by
Methuen & Co Ltd 1961

Copyright © Darrell Waters Ltd 1961

ISBN 0-583-30129-0

Printed and bound in Great Britain by
Collins, Glasgow

Set in Intertype Times

"I do wish old Fatty would buck up and come back from wherever he's staying," said Bets. "We've had almost a week of the holidays without him already – such a waste!"

"He's coming back today," said Pip, passing a post-card across the breakfast-table to his young sister. "Here's a card from him. Three cheers!"

Bets read the card out loud. "Back tomorrow by bus from Warling. Meet me at bus stop if you can. What about a nice juicy mystery? I feel just about ready for one. Fatty."

"A nice juicy *what*?" said her mother, puzzled.

"*Mystery*," said Bets, her eyes shining. "You know how something always seems to happen when Fatty's about, Mother – there was the mystery of the Panto-mime cat – and the mystery of the Vanished Prince – and . . ."

Her father groaned. "Look, Bets – I'm tired of all these adventures and strange happenings that seem to pop up whenever your friend Frederick is about. Just try and steer clear of any trouble these holidays. I was hoping that Frederick was staying away for a nice long time."

"I wish you wouldn't call him Frederick, Daddy," said Bets. "It does sound so silly."

"I should have thought that Frederick was a much better name for a boy in his teens, than the absurd name of Fatty," said her father. "I wonder Frederick allows people to call him by that old nickname now."

"But Fatty *is* fat, and the name suits him," said Pip. "Anyway I don't think *my* nickname is very suitable

5

for me now that I'm a bit older. Why can't I be called by my proper name of Philip, instead of Pip?"

"Simply because you're a bit of pip-squeak still and probably always will be," said his father, disappearing behind his newspaper. Bets gave a sudden laugh, and then a groan as Pip kicked her under the table.

"Pip!" said his mother warningly. Bets changed the subject hurriedly. She didn't want Pip to get into any trouble the very day that Fatty came home.

"Mother, where's the bus time-table?" she said. "I'd like to find out what time old Fatty's bus arrives."

"Well, seeing that there are only two in the morning, and the bus from Warling takes two hours to get here, I should think he'll be on the *first* bus," said Pip, "otherwise he'd be jolly late!"

"It should be about a quarter to ten," said his mother. "That means you'll have plenty of time to clear up the fearful mess in your playroom first. I could hardly get into it yesterday."

Pip groaned. "WHY do we always have to tidy the playroom when we plan to go out?" he demanded. "I really do think it's . . ."

"Enough said," said his father, from behind his newspaper, and Pip became silent at once. He looked across at Bets, and she grinned at him happily. Fatty was coming back! Fatty with his wide grin, his twinkling eyes, his mad jokes – and his extraordinary habit of suddenly finding himself in the middle of peculiar mysteries! Oh the time they had had with Fatty – the excitement – the adventures! Why was it that some people *always* found themselves in the middle of something thrilling?

"If Fatty was cast away on a lonely desert island something extraordinary would immediately happen," thought Bets. "A mermaid would pop up and let him swim away on her back. Or a submarine might arrive and . . ."

"Bets, what are you dreaming about?" said her mother. "You've carefully buttered your bread on *both* sides!"

Pip and Bets tore upstairs as soon as breakfast was finished, only one thought on their minds – Fatty was coming back! "Let's buck up and tidy the playroom," said Pip. "I want to go round to Larry's and see if he and Daisy know that Fatty's coming back today."

He began to throw everything into the big toy cupboard, higgledy, piggledy, bang, crash, wallop!

"Mother won't like that," began Bets, but Pip only laughed at her. "All right – *you* do it properly, old slowcoach. Goodbye – I'm off to Larry's. See you later!"

But Bets couldn't bear to be left behind, so she shoved in the last few things, flew to get her hat and raced down the stairs after Pip, falling over the cat sitting on the bottom stair.

"Sorry, Puss!" she panted, and raced down to the front gate. "Pip! WAIT for me!"

Soon they were at Larry's house. The front door was open, and they could hear Daisy calling to her brother. "Aren't you ready to meet Fatty? You'll be late!"

In a few moments all four children were on their way to the bus-stop. "What do you bet that old Fatty will play one of his tricks on us, and come in some kind of disguise?" said Pip.

"Well, I hope he does," said Larry. "We'd soon see through it. Fatty can't disguise his plumpness!"

"Look, we're *just* in time," said Bets. "Here comes the bus. Let's run!"

The bus, a double-decker, came to a stop, and the four children ran to the exit at the back. People were crowding off, and the conductor was shouting loudly, "Hurry off, please, and mind the step!"

Larry suddenly nudged Pip. "Look, that's Fatty – he's disguised himself, just as we guessed he would.

7

He's carrying a dog-basket too, and I bet old dog Buster is in there. Stand back – don't let him see us!"

The fellow who was carrying the dog-basket was stout, and wore a bulky overcoat, a yellow scarf round his neck and chin, and a cap with a large peak pulled down over his nose. He coughed hollowly as he stepped down from the bus, and held a large green cotton handkerchief to his mouth.

Bets giggled. "That's Fatty all right!" she said in a low voice to Pip. "Let's not say a word, but just follow him solemnly home!"

They set off, keeping just behind him. The fat fellow went off at quite a pace, limping slightly with his left foot.

"Yes, that's Fatty!" said Larry. "Sort of thing he *would* do, in disguise – put on a limp or something! He can't fool *us*, though!"

They followed the limping youth down the street, round a corner and up the hill. Then Larry shouted to him.

"Hey, Fatty! Stop! We know it's you!"

The youth swung round and glared at them. "Don't you dare to call after *me*!" he shouted. "Cheeky young brats!"

"Go on, Fatty – we can't *help* knowing it's you!" said Pip. "And we know you've got old Buster-dog in that basket, too. Let him out!"

"Buster? Who's Buster?" said the fellow. "Are you mad? There's a *cat* in here, not a dog! Have a look!"

He slipped the catch of the basket, and opened the lid. Out sprang a most enormous ginger cat, spitting and hissing!

The four children stared in the greatest astonishment. A CAT – not Buster! So this fellow *wasn't* Fatty after all. Gosh – what an awful mistake!

"Er – we're very sorry. It's all a mistake," stuttered

poor Larry, his face scarlet. "We do beg your pardon."

"Now you just listen to me," said the fat fellow, angrily. "See that bobby over there? Well, I'm going to complain of you, see? Following me about! Whispering behind my back. Calling me names! I can't help being fat, can I? Come here, Pussykins – that's right, you hiss at these little varmints. Scratch them if you like!"

To the children's horror, the fellow went across the road to a corner – and who should be standing there but Mr. Goon, the village policeman. Mr. GOON! He was no friend of theirs! What in the world could they do?

"Better get away quickly, before Mr. Goon comes after us!" said Pip. "Gosh – what a mistake we made!"

He turned to run, and bumped hard into someone standing just behind him, grinning, a little Scottie dog in his arms.

"FATTY! It's you! Fatty, we thought you were that fellow over there, with the dog-basket!" cried Pip, overjoyed to see his friend gain. "We followed him, and now he's gone to complain about us to Goon!"

"And *I* followed *you*!" said Fatty. "I was on the top deck of the bus, and I saw you, though you didn't see me! I carried Buster because I was afraid he'd go careering after you, and give the game away. Give your friends a lick, Buster!"

He held up the little Scottie, and Buster most ecstatically licked all his four friends, whining in joy. Then Fatty put him down on the pavement, and alas, Buster suddenly spotted Goon the policeman, who was staring angrily at the children from across the road.

Buster gave a yelp of delight and raced across the road at top speed. Ah, here was his old enemy! What about dancing round his ankles and pretending to nip him? Buster felt just like a little exercise after his long ride on the bus!

9

Mr. Goon glared at the excited Buster in disgust. "Ha – you little pest of a dog! So you're back with your master, are you? Get away, now! Clear-orf!"

"Buster's only telling you how pleased he is to see you," said Fatty, as the burly policeman tried to skip away from Buster's attentions. "My word, Mr. Goon, you ought to learn dancing! You're really nippy with your feet – almost as nippy as Buster is with his teeth! Heel, Buster! The Dancing Lesson is over!"

Goon went purple in the face. That boy! That toad of a boy! What wonderful peace and quiet there had been in the village for at least a week, with That Boy away! Now he was back, and something would turn up to make things uncomfortable, Goon was sure. That fat boy was always in the middle of Peculiar Happenings of some sort!

Fatty joined the others, who feeling sure that the fellow with the cat had complained about them to Mr. Goon, were keeping well away from the angry policeman.

"I must say that I think you were all a bit fatheaded – following a chap-with-a-cat instead of a boy-with-a-dog," said Fatty.

"All right – don't rub it in," said Larry. "I'll stand us all ice-creams to make up for our mistake."

"Sorry – but I think I *must* get home first," said Fatty. "Mother will be looking out for me. But let's have a Meeting this afternoon – A Meeting of the Famous Find-Outers and Dog! Come to my workroom about half-past two. Come on, Buster old thing! To heel! and DO remember to be polite and shake paws with my father and mother as SOON as you see them!"

Larry and Daisy went off together and so did Pip and Bets. Bets' mother was amused to see the little girl's happy face. "I can see that you met Frederick all right!" she said.

"We're having a Meeting at Fatty's this afternoon," said Bets, her face glowing. "It's the first Meeting the Find-Outers have had for ages!"

"Find-Outers?" said her mother. "Let me see now, that's ..."

"Oh, *Mother*! You *know* we're the Five Find-Outers – and Dog!" said Pip. "Don't you remember all the mysteries we've solved? I daresay we'll find out another and solve it *these* hols!"

"*If* one turns up!" said Bets.

Don't worry, Bets. Things always happen when Fatty is around. I don't expect you will have to wait *very* long before a nice "juicy" mystery looms up for every one of you!

Down in Fatty's Workroom

Bets felt excited when at last the time came to go to the first Meeting of the holidays. Her mother had not allowed her to race off immediately after dinner, but had sent both her and Pip up to their playroom.

"I don't know if you think that what you did this morning to tidy up the room was anything *like* enough," she said. "Throwing things higgledy-piggledy into corners and cupboards isn't *my* idea of clearing up. Please do the job properly before you go!"

"Oh *blow*!" said Pip, exasperated. "Now we shall be late. Come on, Bets, you do your share."

It was soon done, and they raced off down the garden path, happy to be on their way to Fatty's house. They joined up with Larry and Daisy, and were soon in Fatty's workroom at the bottom of his garden, well away from everyone, and *almost* out of range of any shout from the house!

11

"Grown-ups want an awful lot of things done if you're within shouting distance, you know," Fatty said. "But if they have to go and *fetch* you, they're sure to decide it's too much bother – so they do the things themselves!"

The shed was certainly well tucked away, and very, very comfortable. An oil-stove gave quite enough warmth and on the floor was an old tiger-skin complete with its head. Bets had been scared at first of its open mouth, showing such fierce teeth, and of its glassy eyes – but now she didn't mind it a bit, and often sat on the great head itself.

"This tiger is getting a bit moth-eaten," she said. "We ought to powder him – that's what Mother does to *our* fur-rugs. Oh, Fatty – you've still got the old crocodile skin stretched on the wall too. I do think this is a most exciting shed. It's lovely to be back again, after so long at school."

"Nice to have you here, little Bets," said Fatty, in the "special" voice he sometimes kept for the little girl. "Be careful the old tiger doesn't nip you!"

"Woof," said Buster at once, and showed his teeth.

"He says *he'd* nip the tiger if he did a thing like that!" said Bets, and cuddled Buster round the neck.

"Got anything to eat, Fatty?" asked Larry. "I had quite a good dinner, but somehow I always feel hungry when we meet down here."

"There are some chocolate biscuits in the cupboard," said Fatty, who invariably seemed to be provided with a vast variety of good food, wherever he was. "By the way, please look firmly the other way if Buster tries to beg any food from you. He is on a diet – slimming, you know. He over-ate himself while he was away. Too many cats about!"

"But surely he hasn't begun to eat *cats*!" said Daisy, shocked.

"No, ass! But with plenty of cat-dishes around always ready to be licked clean, he did far too well," said Fatty. "Buster, stand up. Show your tubby figure – oh what a middle you've landed yourself with – disgraceful!"

Buster certainly had a tummy. His tail dropped when Fatty scolded him, and he went sadly into a corner and curled himself up, eyeing the chocolate biscuits sadly. Bets felt very sorry for him. "I'll just let him *lick* my chocolatey fingers, Fatty," she said. "That's all, I promise. I just can't bear to see him looking so left-out. Here you are, Buster – lick my fingers."

Buster was pleased. He licked Bets' fingers and then sat down as close to her as he possibly could. He loved kind-hearted little Bets. She put her arm round him again.

"Fatty – is this meeting about anything special?" she said. "I'd be just as pleased if there wasn't any Mystery to solve at the moment, I mean – I do like mysteries, but I do like a bit of peace, too."

"Well, really, Bets – don't you *want* to belong to the Find-Outers?" said Daisy, quite amazed. "What's the good of being a Find-Outer if you don't want to find out anything?"

"Yes, I see all that," said Bets. "But what I mean is – do we *have* to snoop round and look for problems and mysteries to solve – can't we just not bother for once?"

"You mean – just play about and enjoy ourselves?" said Daisy. "Well – it does sound rather nice for a change. You know, Fatty, solving mysteries *can* be quite hard work."

"Well, I'm rather inclined to agree with you," said Fatty, lazily. "You know, I've just been staying with two cousins – both first-class footballers – first-class boxers – first-class cross-country runners – and first-class bores, to tell you the truth! My word, the excuses I had to think of to get out of kicking a football from

13

morning to night – running for miles in shorts uphill and down – and putting on boxing-gloves and having sparring bouts. Thank goodness *that* didn't last long – the sparring, I mean."

"Why – were you knocked out?" asked Larry.

"Knocked out! Don't be fatheaded," said Fatty. "The tiring part about the boxing was that *I* kept on doing the knocking-out – I tell you, it got boring!"

"You're boasting, Fatty," said Larry. "Ha – you'll never get rid of *that* habit! That's one thing you do better than any of us – boast! You're superlative at that!"

"Don't be rude, Larry!" said Daisy, shocked. "Why, Fatty might knock *you* out, if you talk like that!"

"No, I shan't," said Fatty. "Larry's quite right. I do boast just a bit. On the other hand, I do actually do what I boast about. I really *did* knock out my two cousins. I'll show you the blow I used. You swing out like this with your left, and then – ooh, sorry, Buster! What on earth made you get in the way? Did I hurt you?"

"Funny – you didn't even knock him out," said Larry irritatingly. Bets cuddled poor Buster, who had received a blow on his fat tummy that had quite winded him. He stared at Fatty unhappily, really puzzled.

"Listen," said Pip. "Let's go exploring a bit these hols. My father made a list of interesting spots we could go to see. He said we shouldn't just mess about doing nothing, he said . . ."

"He *said* that – but what he really meant was that he didn't want you under his feet all the time," said Larry. "My father's like that too – I mean, he's an absolute sport, and I'm frightfully proud of him – and he is of me – but I do notice that after about ten days of the hols he always gets this idea of us going off for the day – not just one day, but every day. And *mine* made out a list too – here it is. I'll read it out."

He took a neatly written list from the pocket of his

flannels and read from it. "Old Water-Caves at Chiller-bing. Museum of Age-Old Fossils at Tybolds. Norman Tower at Yellow Moss . . ."

"Gosh – those are down on *my* list too!" said Pip, scrabbling in his pocket for it. "Yes – all those are down – and two or three more. Roman Remains at Jackling Museum. Sea-pictures at Banshee Towers, at the top of Banshee Hill. Old Musical Instruments at . . ."

"I don't want to see *any* of them!" said Bets, suddenly looking very woebegone. "I wouldn't so much mind the sea-pictures – I like sea-pictures – but I don't like those ugly fossily things, or those . . ."

"All right, Bets – you shan't spend lovely spring days in Museums or Norman Towers or Caves," said Fatty putting his arm round her. "But we might go and see Banshee Towers. You know why it's called that, don't you?"

Nobody knew. "Well," said Fatty, "a banshee means 'a woman of the fairies' – and it shrieks and wails when any misfortune or unhappiness comes to the family in whose house it lives."

"How very unpleasant," said Daisy, at once. "I'm very glad *my* family doesn't own a banshee. I should be scared stiff. Does Banshee Towers own a banshee, then?"

"I suppose it did once, when the family lived in it," said Fatty. "But now that it's a museum – or a picture-gallery or something – I expect the banshee has retired!"

"I don't want to go to see Banshee Towers if the banshee still lives there," said Bets, decidedly. "So you'll have to find out, Fatty."

"I honestly shouldn't worry," said Fatty. "It would be a pity to let an old-time 'woman of the fairies' frighten you from seeing wonderful sea-pictures. And I believe they really *are* wonderful!"

15

"Well, we'll make a few expeditions to show our parents that we really are not the lie-abeds they think we are," said Larry. "It should be rather fun, actually. We could picnic in these places – and I could use one of them for my holiday essay. It would be something to write about – especially the banshee howling. I hope it wails like anything when we're there!"

"I shan't go if it does," said Bets at once. "Hallo – who's that at the door? Golly, that loud knock made me jump!"

"Who's there?" demanded Fatty.

"It's me – Ern," said a well-known voice outside. "I've been sent to stay with my Uncle Theo – Mr. Goon, you know – because one of my sisters has measles and I haven't had it – at least, Mum can't *remember* me having it. Can I come in?"

"Of course! Come along in, Ern, we're all here," said Fatty, and opened the door. Ern stood there, shock-headed as ever and as plump as Fatty, grinning in delight to see his friends again. Buster at once made a great fuss of him.

"Coo, it's nice to see you all again," said Ern, sitting down on the floor and hugging the little Scottie. "I didn't want to come and stay with my uncle – I don't like him and he doesn't like me – but I don't mind putting up with him if you'll let me be with you now and again. Any mysteries going?"

"Not so far, Ern," said Fatty. "Help yourself to the chocolate biscuits, but DON'T give Buster any. He's slimming."

"Luvaduck – is he really?" said Ern. "I must say he feels a bit solid-like. You look a bit balloony too, Fatty."

"Ern – please remember your manners," said Fatty, in a shocked voice. "You must *not* refer to people as 'balloony'. You might easily get a smack on the nose."

16

"Oooh, I'm sorry, Fatty, *reeeely* sorry," said Ern.

"Maybe I'll pick up a few good manners now I'm with you again. I seem to lose them, like, at 'ome. Er – I mean HOME."

"It's good to see you, Ern," said Fatty. "We are planning to go on some interesting rambles – and you shall come with us, if you like – if your uncle will let you."

"Coo – I'd like that!" said Ern. "Well, Uncle says I've got to Turn To and Look Nippy, and Not get Under His Feet, and Use my Loaf . . ."

"Your *loaf*?" said Bets, in surprise. "Do you have a loaf of bread of your own, then?"

"You don't know much, do you?" grinned Ern, so delighted to be with his old friend again that his eyes shone like stars. "Using your 'Loaf' means using your brains, see?"

"Ah yes," said Fatty, gravely. "Well if we all intend to go sight-seeing and learning about Banshees and Old Musical Instruments, and Roman Remains, we must ALL use our – er – loaves. Are we allowed any butter with them, Ern?"

But dear old Ern didn't see the joke, though the others roared in delight. Ern didn't mind. It was sheer happiness to him to be with Fatty, Bets, and the rest. They could pull his leg, correct him, laugh at him – they were his friends and he was theirs. Let them do whatever they liked, as long as he could be with them!

Bingo – and Buster!

It was fun to have Ern again. He enjoyed the company of the five friends so much, and entered into everything with the greatest delight. He sat listening intently as they

17

went on discussing their plans for the next two or three weeks.

"I suppose I couldn't come with you sometimes?" he said, at last. "I daresay Uncle would let me off now and again. So long as I do the jobs he sets me, of course."

"Yes, if he's kind enough to have you to stay, you must certainly help him in any way you can," said Fatty "His garden, for instance. I passed it the other day – shocking! Full of weeds!"

"That's what my uncle said," agreed Ern, mournfully. "Trouble is – I dunno weeds from flowers. Oh, and there's another thing – he's letting me have my dog with me while I'm here. What do you think of *that*?"

"*Dog?* I didn't even know you had one, Ern," said Pip surprised.

"Well, he's a bit new, like," said Ern. "I've had him for three weeks. I'm trying to train him good and proper – like you've trained old Buster there, Fatty."

"Good!" said Fatty. "Very good. An untrained dog is a nuisance – nobody likes him. Where is this dog of yours – and what's he called? What kind is he?"

"I don't rightly know what kind he is," said Ern. "He's a bit of a mixture really; he's not very big – but he's got a mighty long tail with a mighty big wag in it – and nice ears that prick up like Buster's here – and rather short legs. Pity about his legs, really – he looks comic when he runs, you see, and all the other dogs laugh at him."

"They don't!" said Bets disbelievingly.

"Well they stand and stare at him, and sort of wink at one another when he comes scuttering by," said Ern. "His name is Bingo – good name, isn't it? It suits him too – you wait till you've seen him. I like him an awful lot – it's the first time I've had a dog of my own. He's potty on me you know – thinks I'm the world's wonder!"

"Just like old Buster then," said Bets. "He thinks Fatty's the world's wonder, don't you Buster?"

"Woof!" said Buster, agreeing heartily. He went to Fatty and licked his chin, and then put his head on Fatty's knee, looking up at him adoringly.

"Loving old thing," said Fatty, and patted him. "Well Ern, I'm awfully glad you've a dog of your own. Good for the dog – and good for you, too. You'll like having someone who looks up to you and thinks that everything you do is right! But look after him well, won't you?"

"Where is this Bingo?" asked Larry.

"I've locked him in the wood-shed at Uncle's," said Ern. "You see – well, I didn't know if you'd like me to bring him along. Buster mightn't like him."

"Rubbish!" said Fatty, getting up. "Any dog is a friend of Buster's if he belongs to one of us. Let's go and visit this dog of yours and take him for a walk."

"You're a real sport, Fatty," said Ern, his face glowing. "Come on, then."

They all went out of the shed and made their way to Peterswood Village. Buster dancing round in joy, sniffing along the hedges, barking at a sparrow, wagging his tail without a stop.

"Is your uncle in a good temper today?" enquired Larry.

"So-so," said Ern, with a grin. "He smiled when I cleaned his big boots for him – and he frowned when I upset the milk. He doesn't know I've come to see you."

"Why didn't you tell him?" asked Bets. "You're not *scared* of him, are you?"

"Oh, I'm proper scared of Uncle all right," said Ern. "Bit too free with his hands, he is. I'd like to have sixpence for every slap he's given me – I'd be rich by now – *swimming* in sixpences! I don't think he'll be too pleased if I go about with you too much, so I shan't tell him anything."

19

They came to Goon's little house, which stood not far from the police station. As soon as they opened the gate a terrific volley of blood-curdling howls greeted them, and something hurled itself against the wood-shed door.

"That's him – that's Bingo," said Ern, in pride. "I hope Uncle's out. He wouldn't like that noise at all. Hey, Bingo! I've brought friends to see you."

Buster the Scottie was astonished and rather alarmed to hear the extraordinary noise from the shed. He put his head on one side and pricked up his ears to sharp points. He gave a little growl.

"It's all right, Buster," said Ern. "That's my dog in there. Hey, Bingo, come along out!" And he slipped the catch of the door and opened it.

Out shot something at sixty miles an hour, gave one horrified look at the crowd of children, and disappeared at top speed through the gate.

"That's him!" said Ern, proudly, as Bingo shot down the road. "What do you think of him, Fatty?"

"Well, I really only caught sight of his tail," said Fatty. "But that certainly looked fine. Look out, here comes old Goon – your uncle, Ern. He looks pretty bad-tempered too."

Mr. Goon had opened his front door, and was standing there in his uniform, helmet and all, glaring in his best manner.

"ERN! What's the matter with that dog of yours, barking like that? Has he gone mad or something? Where is he?"

"I don't know Uncle," said Ern, truthfully. "He shot off at top speed. I only hope he hasn't gone back to my home. He might catch measles, and come out in nasty spots."

"You and your measles!" snorted Mr. Goon. "I said you could have that dog if he behaved himself – and if

20

I could borrow him at nights when I go down into the rough part of the town; but I tell you this straight, Ern – if he's going to act silly, and bark at nothing, and rush off like a mad thing, I won't have him. And you might tell him to keep away from my feet. He's tripped me up twice already."

"Oh, I'm very sorry about that, Uncle," said Ern. "Er – I just brought my friends to see him."

"Well, you can take them away again," said Goon, ungraciously. "They may be your friends, but they're not *mine* – especially Master Frederick Algernon Trotteville – pah!"

"Who's he talking about?" said Ern, in wonder, as Goon went indoors and slammed the door.

"Me, I'm afraid," said Fatty. "Those are my real names, you know, Ern. I try to forget them, though I can't say I like my nickname either. Now – what about your dog Bingo, Ern? Where do you suppose he's gone?"

"I don't know," said Ern, suddenly looking desperate. "I can't think why he went off like that. I suppose my uncle went and shouted at him in the shed and gave him a lamming or something. Let's go and look for him."

But before they had gone more than a few steps, Mr. Goon was at his door again, shouting for Ern.

"Ern! You come back! What about those jobs I gave you to do? You come back, I tell you."

"Better go, Ern," said Fatty. "Cheer up. We'll have a look for old Bingo. He won't have come to any harm."

Ern went slowly back through the gate, looking angry and troubled. His thoughts were full of Bingo, his beloved dog. He might get run over! He might get lost! He might even be stolen. "He's so friendly and good-natured, he would go with anyone," thought poor Ern, and began to run as he heard a stentorian shout from inside the house.

21

"ERN! You come on IN! I've got to go to the police station, and I want you to peel the potatoes for supper and get things tidy. ERN!"

Poor Ern disappeared into the house. He longed to slam the door, just as Goon had done, but he didn't dare.

The others walked slowly through the village, talking about Ern, and keeping a look-out for Bingo. There was no sign of him. Fatty thought he must have gone to find his way back to Ern's own home. They decided to go to the bun-shop and have tea there. Buster was pleased. He knew that this usually meant a few tit-bits for him!

Just as they reached the bun-shop they heard a little whine – a very small and pathetic one. It seemed to come from the hedge nearby. Buster went at once to investigate. He slipped through the hedge and then gave a sharp bark.

"Buster – what is it? Come back!" called Fatty. Buster appeared again – with something trotting behind him – Bingo!

"BINGO!" said everyone, in astonishment, and Bingo wagged his long tail, went flat on his tummy, and began to crawl anxiously towards them, in a most humble manner.

"Poor Bingo!" said Bets, in her gentle voice, and at once Bingo shot over to her, pressed himself against her and gave a funny little high whine. He wagged his long tail so hard that it slapped against Bets' legs, but she didn't mind. She patted him and stroked him, and he went nearly mad with joy. Buster stood nearby and watched gravely.

"Well – you're a bit of a comic, Bingo, I must say," said Fatty, looking at him from all angles. "What a tail! Pity you didn't have legs to match, old boy! But my word, you've real doggy eyes!"

22

Yes, Bingo had good, bright, faithful eyes, and a tongue always ready to lick any friend. The children decided that Ern was lucky. "What do *you* think of him, Buster?" said Fatty, seeing Buster standing and watching everything, his eyes bright, his tail wagging just a very little.

"Woof," said Buster, and went straight over to Bingo. He stood nose to nose with him, each sniffing at the other. Then Buster danced round Bingo, and Bingo gave a joyful bark, and away they went together, tearing down the road like mad things!

"Buster approves," said Larry. "*I* rather approve of him too. A comical dog, but a real little sport. Well, if we're going to have tea at the bun-shop, what about it? And please don't eat more than six buns, Fatty – you want to be able to squeeze out of the door again!"

In they all went, made for their favourite table, and sat down. Fatty, as usual, had plenty of money, and that meant a good tuck-in for everyone. In the middle of the meal, the door was pushed open with a heave, and in trotted the two dogs, panting, their mouths open as if they were both laughing!

"Buster – go and shut the door after you," said Fatty sternly. "Have you forgotten your manners? Bingo, please notice that doors must be pushed shut, not left open, when you come in and out of rooms."

"Wuff," said Bingo, head on one side, listening carefully. He trotted over to the door and helped Buster to shut it, using both paws and nose.

"He's 'One of Us' already!" said Larry. "I'm beginning to like you Bingo, old thing. Now *sit*! Buster, teach him how to sit. Gosh, look at that, Fatty – both sitting down side by side, as good as gold! We're going to have some fun with old Bingo!"

Mr Goon loses his temper

Ern had been very busy indeed while the others had gone to the village. Mr. Goon was in one of his worst tempers. He always was when he had met Fatty, whom he disliked very much.

"That fat boy!" he said to Ern. "I don't trust him an inch. Never did. It's a pity he's not as stupid as he looks. Too clever by half, he is!"

"He *doesn't* look stupid, Uncle," said Ern, emptying some potatoes into a bowl of water to peel. "How could he when he's got such marvellous brains! You should hear him talk – luvaduck, he knows pretty well everything!"

"I'll luvaduck you if you don't get on with those potatoes, Ern," said Mr. Goon. "That fat boy's a menace – yes, that's the word for him – a menace!"

"What's a menace, Uncle?" asked Ern. "Anything to do with manners? Sounds a bit the same."

"I don't know if you're being rude, or just plain stupid, Ern," said Mr. Goon majestically. "But this I do know – you'll get a clip on the ear soon."

"And one of these days my dog will bite you if you clip me!" cried Ern, almost at the end of his tether. "Now Uncle – don't you come any nearer. I'll throw this bowl of potatoes over you, if you do!"

Ern looked so fierce that Goon retreated hurriedly. "Now, now," he said, "don't take things so seriously, Ern. Can't you see a joke?"

"Depends who makes it," said Ern, feeling suddenly victorious. then his spirits fell again as he remembered his dog. Where *was* old Bingo? Had he run away for

ever? He sniffed a little as he went on peeling the potatoes, and when he remembered how Bingo ran to meet
him and licked him lovingly each time he came home
from school, a tear fell plop into the potato bowl.

"I'm a fathead – that's what Fatty would call me,"
thought Ern. "But I dunno – there's something about a
dog that gets you – specially if it's your own."

Mr. Goon went off to the police station, his boots
well polished by Ern, and his helmet and uniform well
brushed. Ern was glad to see him go. As soon as his
uncle was out of sight he thought he would whistle for
Bingo – just to see if by *any* chance he would come.

So he whistled. Ern had a most piercing whistle, shrill,
long and alarming. It made everyone within hearing
jump in surprise and annoyance. Ern stood at the front
gate and whistled for at least five minutes. No Bingo
arrived – but a good many windows and doors were
opened, and people began looking out to see if anything was the matter. They thought that it must be Goon
blowing his police-whistle for help !

A small boy arrived, panting, at the front gate, "Any
help wanted?" he asked. "We heard the police-whistle
being blown."

"That was only me whistling for my dog," said Ern,
astonished. Then, seeing people looking out of windows
and doors, he shot inside Goon's house in a hurry.
"They'll tell Uncle I was using his police-whistle," he
thought desperately. "Luvaduck, what a day ! Wish I
was at home, measles and all !"

About half-past five Mr. Goon returned home to see
if Ern had put on the kettle and had made him some
toast, as he had commanded. Fortunately for Ern, he
had everything ready. Ern was right down in the
dumps: no Fatty had come back, no Buster, no Bets –
and certainly no Bingo. Ern didn't want any tea at all,
a most unusual thing.

"This toast is burnt," said Mr. Goon grumpily.

"It's not," said Ern. "It's just right. That's how my Ma likes it, anyway."

"And you've put too much tea in the pot," said Mr. Goon, peering in, holding the lid in his hand. It was hot and he had to drop it very suddenly. It fell to the floor and broke. He glared at Ern as if *he* had dropped it!

Ern gave a sudden giggle, and his uncle went red in the face. "Pick them pieces up," he commanded, "and take that grin off your face, Ern."

"I can't. It's stuck there," said Ern, suddenly feeling cheeky.

"ERN!" said Mr. Goon, in a terrifying voice, and stood up. Ern promptly stood up too, and ran to the door. He opened it and Goon came after him. Ern went down the hall to the front door and opened that, and then shot down the front path with his uncle on his heels – at exactly the same moment as Fatty and the rest, with Buster and Bingo, came in at the gate.

Somehow or other Mr. Goon became mixed up with the two excited dogs as they raced towards the front door – and down he went with a thud. Bingo leapt up at the astonished Ern, and tried his hardest to lick him in as many places as he could, barking madly all the time. Buster, finding his old enemy, Goon, on the ground, and at his mercy, sailed in gleefully to the attack! It really was a sight to be seen!

"BINGO! You've come back!" shouted Ern in joy, and lifted up the delighted dog, who at once plastered his face with loving licks

"CLEAR ORF, ALL OF YOU!" roared poor Mr. Goon, trying to push Buster away. "I'll tell your parents of this! WILL you order this dog away, Frederick Trotteville? One of these days I'll clap you in a cell, yes, and the dog too. Get away, you brute! Lemme get up! Ern help me up."

26

"Clear orf, all of you!" roared Mr. Goon.

It was Fatty who pulled the heavy policeman to his feet and dusted him down, murmuring apologies in a polite voice that simply infuriated Mr. Goon!

"Bad luck, sir! Did you trip over your feet? I say, you'll scare the girls, if you roar like that. Buster, behave yourself. BUSTER! Are you deaf? Stop dancing round poor Mr. Goon. Here, let me help you up, sir – up we come – that's it – upsadaisy. You all right now, Mr. Goon?"

Mr. Goon glared. He saw that quite a crowd had gathered round his front gate – and some of them were daring to laugh! Laughing at the Law! What were things coming to? Most majestically Mr. Goon went to the gate and scowled at everyone there. "What's all this? Clear orf, now! You're creating a nuisance, you are. Move on, there, MOVE ON!"

Only a few people moved away, Fatty felt sorry for poor Mr. Goon. "Perhaps if you told them to Move OFF instead of Move ON, they'd understand better," he suggested "Let me help you, Mr. Goon." And Fatty waved an imperious hand and shouted in a suddenly enormous voice, "MOVE OFF, WILL YOU! MOVE OFF!"

And, rather astonished, the lookers-on moved off at once. Fatty was rather astonished too – he hadn't thought it would be so easy! Mr. Goon was more than astonished. He was exceedingly angry.

"Think you're in the police force now, do you?" he said, fiercely. "Well, what about you Moving Off – *or* on – I don't care which. Funny how trouble always comes when you're about, isn't it, Master Trotteville? Now I'm going back to finish my tea in peace and quiet. Clear orf, all of you! I'm sick of the sight of you. You get indoors, Ern – and take that dog to the woodshed. Tripping me up like that. You can consider him arrested and put into a cell, see? And there he'll stay out in the wood-shed, night and day!"

"Oh *no*, Uncle – that would be cruel!" said Ern, upset. "Fatty, tell him. He might listen to you. You can't lock up a dog, night and day."

"All right then, you go home!" stormed Mr. Goon. "I do a kindness and take you in – and that fatheaded dog too – and this is what happens. Go on home! Catch the measles!"

Ern didn't know what to do – but Fatty did. He whispered something in Ern's ear, and Ern's face broke into a delighted smile. He took hold of Fatty's hand and shook it hard. "You're a friend, Fatty – yes, that's what you are, a friend," said Ern warmly. "I'll go and get my things straightaway. Would you mind Bingo for me, till I come out? Uncle's in such a temper, he might whip him. WHAT a pity he tripped over Bingo!"

Bets and Daisy had been very scared by all the upset, but the boys had rather enjoyed it. Fatty couldn't help feeling a little sorry for Mr. Goon. The policeman did not shine when things went wrong; but Fatty felt sure he would be sorry and feel guilty when he had had time to ponder over things. That was the worst of a hot temper – it led you into doing silly, rash things you were sorry for afterwards – and then it was probably too late.

Ern had disappeared into his uncle's house. He was there about three minutes and then came out again, carrying a canvas bag. Bingo trotted joyfully over to him. Ern was beaming all over his round face.

"Where are you going, Ern?" asked Bets, in surprise. "Home? But you can't go there, with measles about!"

They all went out of the gate together, leaving Mr. Goon staring after them. He was just beginning to wish that he hadn't lost his temper.

"Ern, come back! You come and apologize and I'll let you stay!" he shouted.

"Sorry, Uncle," shouted back Ern. "I can't stay where

I'm not wanted – or where my dog will be locked up night and day. Sorry, Uncle!"

"Where's Ern going?" asked Pip.

"He's going to stay in my workroom till his family are clear of the measles," said Fatty. "*And* Bingo as well. Nice dog, Bingo. Be good for Buster to have company too. The workroom is nice and warm, and I can put a camp-bed there. But nobody is to know, see? You are all to Keep Your Mouths Shut. Ern is our friend, and we've got to stand by him."

"Oh *good*, Fatty! You always think of some fine way out of things when they go wrong," said Bets, squeezing Fatty's arm. "Ern, are you pleased?"

"Pleased? I feel like a tail with two dogs," said Ern, looking down at Buster and Bingo trotting amicably together. "No, I mean a dog with two tails. Coo luva-duck – wasn't poor old Uncle in a temper – all because he fell over Bingo! To think I'm going to stay in your workroom. Fatty – I feel honoured, straight I do! You're a friend – and I can't say more than that, can I?"

"No, that's about the best thing anyone can say about anyone else," said Fatty, with one of his grins. He gave Ern a little punch in the back. "I bet I'll say that about *you* someday, Ern!"

Ern glowed. He looked round gratefully at the little bunch of friends walking with him. Yes, that was about the best thing that could happen to anyone – to Have Friends, whether they were two-legged or four-legged.

"And to BE a friend to someone is just as good," thought Ern. "Well – maybe it's even better. I'll have to ask Fatty about it sometime. He's sure to know!"

Fatty is a real friend

The little company went in at the back gate of Fatty's garden, and trooped down to the shed – Fatty's cosy little workroom. The two dogs trotted along amicably together. Bingo occasionally giving Buster a friendly lick. Bingo's tail never stopped wagging or waving.

"You'll wear it out if you're not careful, Bingo." said Ern, as they went in close file down the path, Bingo's tail slapping against the nearest legs. Bets laughed. She didn't feel scared any longer – just pleased and excited. She was glad that Ern had got away from unkind Mr. Goon. It would be nice to have him at their meetings.

The workroom felt warm when they opened the door, and was full of a golden light from the sinking sun.

"Well, here we are once more," said Fatty. "Get out the toffees, Bets – they're in that cupboard. I'll just go up to the house and see if I can find a camp-bed – or a spare mattress, if not."

He disappeared, and Bets went to find the toffees. Trust Fatty to have something to chew or suck or drink! Good old Fatty to think about rescuing poor Ern!

Fatty was in the middle of hunting about for a camp-bed when his mother appeared. She was astonished to see him in the lumber-room. "What in the world do you want, Fatty?" she said.

"Er – well, I just wondered if there was a camp-bed to spare," said Fatty.

"A camp-bed? Whatever for?" said his mother. "Fatty, I will NOT allow you to sleep out in the garden yet! You'd catch your death of cold!"

"Mother dear, I'm not thinking of such a thing!"

31

said Fatty. "I like my own warm bed much too much to want to shiver outside, with beetles and frogs and ants all over me. I just wondered if we *had* a camp-bed to spare, that's all."

"Fatty, why are you so mysterious about it?" asked his mother. "Look at me! Why this sudden idea of a camp-bed?"

"Darling Mother, you are always so curious," said Fatty, taking her hand. "Can't you trust me? I don't want to sleep on it. I don't want to sell it. I don't even want to take it off the premises. I just want to *borrow* it. I'm afraid if I told you *why* I want it, someone might ask you questions and then you'd answer – and someone else might suffer. Please trust me, Mother, and believe that, like the Boy Scouts, I am about to do a Good Deed!"

"I never in my life knew anyone who could wheedle things out of me like you, Frederick," said his mother, beginning to laugh. "All right – I won't ask you any questions. I'll trust you – as I always do, dear! There's a spare camp-bed in the cupboard under the stairs."

"Bless you, Mother, you're a pet," said Fatty, and gave her a smacking kiss on the cheek. He went to the cupboard and found the camp-bed. In no time at all he had carried it down the garden, unseen, and Larry was helping him to take it through the door of the shed.

"Did you have any bother getting it?" asked Larry. "I always have to go into long, long explanations when *I* want to borrow anything like a camp-bed."

"No. Fortunately my mother trusts me as much as I trust *her*," said Fatty, putting up the camp-bed with Ern. "Nothing like trust in a family! I can recommend it thoroughly."

Ern stared at Fatty. What queer things Fatty sometimes said – but they were worth remembering. Ern thought, "Nothing like trust in a family." That meant trusting one another. There was quite a lot in that idea. Ern decided to think about it when he was in bed. He felt excited when he saw the camp-bed neatly made up in a corner of the workroom.

"Luvaduck!" he said. "It's a miracle, this! Me sleeping here, all on my own, safe as houses, and my uncle not knowing a thing about it. I don't know how to thank you enough, Fatty, that I don't."

"Well, don't try," said Fatty. "Bets, did you find the toffees – ah yes, I see a lump in your cheek, and one in Pip's."

"Fatty, can we do anything to help Ern?" asked Bets. "I mean – bring food, or something like that. Cook will always give us bits and pieces."

"Well, I vote we all bring what we can, without arousing any *suspicions*," said Fatty. "Ern had better send a post-card to his mother, saying "Getting on fine, quite happy", or something like that – in case Goon tells her that he's sent Ern off. But I don't somehow think he will! He'll imagine that Ern has rushed back home, with awful tales about him!"

"I'm going to enjoy myself," said Ern, bouncing up and down on the camp-bed. "Wish *I* could do something for somebody – you, Bets, for instance. I'd do anything, reely I would!"

"I've no doubt your chance will come someday," said Fatty. "Now, what about a game? Or shall we first of all decide what expeditions we are going to make this week?"

"It sounds as if we were explorers or something." said Pip. "How nice to be able to say 'What about exploring the Sahara, old man?" Or "I think we should row down the Nile and count the number of crocodiles there, dear fellow'!"

The others chuckled. "Well, let's take a vote of where we should go first," said Fatty, taking two sheets of paper from a shelf. "Here are the lists made out by Pip's father and Larry's – together with a few notes of my own. I think we'll take a vote as to which two places we would prefer to visit. We can always go and see the others afterwards, if we want to."

He read out the list of places. "Well, there you are. Now just choose two of those, each of you, and scribble them down, fold your papers in half and give them to me. I'll open them and see which places the majority of us want to visit."

Soon they were all busy. Bets asked how to spell "Banshee" so everyone at once knew *one* of her choices! The notes were handed to Fatty and he opened them.

"Well, the two places that the majority of you want to see are: the old Water-Caves at Chillerbing – and Banshee Towers on Banshee Hill. Bets, I'm surprised *you* put down Banshee Towers. I thought you'd be scared of any places connected with banshees wailing in the night!"

"Fatty, I only chose Banshee Towers because you said there were magnificent sea-pictures there," said Bets. "I won't go if there are *still* banshees, though – unkind fairies wailing and foretelling horrible things! I'd hate that."

"Dear Bets, banshees only belong to fairy tales," said Fatty, seeing that Bets looked rather scared. "We shan't see or hear a single banshee – but we *shall* see a magnificent set of sea-pictures. I believe some of them reach from floor to ceiling. We shall feel quite seasick if we gaze at them too long."

"I shall take some seasick medicine with me, then," said Bets solemnly. "I've some left – a few pills."

Everyone roared with laughter. "I'm only teasing you Bets," said Fatty. "I say – *do* look at those two dogs!"

They all turned to look – and there were Buster and

Bingo, *both* squeezed into Buster's basket, fast asleep, so entangled that, as Larry said, "T'other couldn't be told from which!" Pip glanced at Fatty and Ern. Both had such pleased, admiring looks on their faces that Pip laughed.

"Look at Fatty and Ern," he said. "Did you ever see such dippy looks on any faces except dog-lovers?"

"Yes, I did – on yours on your birthday when Granny gave you two white rabbits!" said Bets at once. "You looked at them just like Auntie Sue looks when she goes to see if her twins are asleep! *Quite* dippy!"

That made Pip go red, and everyone laughed. "You're getting quite smart, young Bets," said Fatty. "Well, to come back to Banshee Towers. I see that four out of five have voted for that, so we'll go there. And three out of five have voted for the Water-Caves. So those are our first two expeditions."

"*I* voted for Banshee Towers, too," said Ern, to Bets. "I'm mad on sea-pictures. You see, I want to go into the Navy when I'm old enough, so *I* had to vote for the sea-picture place. And don't you worry about banshees, Bets. The moment I see one, I'll whistle like this, see, and I'll make them so scared they'll fly out of the window and never come back!" And Ern suddenly put two fingers into his mouth, screwed up his face, and gave a very sudden, very long and extremely piercing whistle. It made everyone jump violently, and the two dogs in the basket leapt straight up into the air as if they had been shot.

Buster barked and Bingo howled, and both dogs tore round and round the room after imaginary enemies. Ern was quite overcome at the commotion he had caused.

Fatty glared at him. "ERN! Do you want to bring all the policemen in the neighbourhood here? That whistling of yours is EXACTLY like a police-whistle. You'll have my father and my mother down here if you don't look out."

"Luvaduck!" muttered Ern, trying to catch Bingo as he tore past him for the third time, really scared.

Fatty heard a shout from somewhere outside, and groaned. "Somebody is coming!" he said. "Switch off the light, Bets, quick – the switch is just behind you. Shut up barking, Buster, you ass. Now – no noise, anyone. We'll sit here in the dark and hope nobody comes to find out what on earth we are doing here. SHHHHHHH!"

Not a sound was to be heard in the darkened room except some rather heavy breathing from a scared Ern. Suppose he was found here by his uncle or somebody and sent home? Ern wished and wished that he hadn't shown Bets how he proposed to frighten a banshee.

After five minutes had ticked by, Fatty judged it safe to put on the lights again. As he did so, there came the sound of a gong from his house, away up the garden. He groaned.

"That's my supper bell. Where *has* the evening gone to? I'll have to go. You and Pip ought to go too, Bets."

"Gosh, and so had we!" said Larry, pulling Daisy to her feet. "Good thing our father and mother are out tonight, and there's only Cookie to see us. Goodnight everyone. Sleep well, Ern. So long, Bingo-dog. Be good!"

"Wuff," said Bingo, pleased to hear his name. He accompanied everyone to the door, his tail wagging nineteen to the dozen. The two dogs gave each other a quick lick, and Buster trotted up the garden with Fatty.

Ern was left alone in the shed. He was astonished to hear Bingo growling softly twenty minutes later, and horrified to hear soft foot-steps coming to the door. His heart sank. Was it his uncle coming to fetch him? But how could he *possibly* know where he, Ern, was? The door opened and a torch shone in, lighting up the

"Fatty, the turnstile man is coming back!"

darkness in which Ern sat. Ern trembled and shook, feeling most alarmed.

"Ern! It's me, Fatty. I've come to bring you some supper – and to tell you there's a torch in the table drawer, if you want to see to eat or to read. I shan't be able to come down again to the shed tonight, so goodnight, and sleep well. I'll bring you some breakfast in the morning."

"Coo, thanks, you're a wonder, Fatty," said the grateful Ern, and took the tray that Fatty handed in.

"There's a bone for old Bingo, from Buster," said Fatty, giving him a paper bag. "So long, Ern. See you tomorrow!"

"So long," said Ern, gratefully, and sat down to eat a nice piece of fried fish, mashed potatoes and greens. He gave the bone to Bingo, who was thrilled. He made such a noise gnawing it that Ern felt sure it could be heard for miles around!

"Bingo, old dog – are you enjoying this?" said Ern when at last he had undressed and slipped under the rug that Fatty had left for the camp-bed. "Come on under the rug with me – we'll keep each other warm. That's right. Snuggle down. Goodnight!"

Goodnight, Ern and Bingo. You're quite safe, though Somebody has peeped in at the window, and knows you are there! Don't worry: it was only the black cat next door – and she fled as soon as she saw Bingo! Sleep tight!

Off to Banshee Hill

Ern had a happy, but very restless night. Bingo kept imagining that he heard rats running round outside the shed, trying to get in, and leapt on and off the camp-bed every few minutes, rushing to sniff round the corners of the shed, his long tail waving in excitement.

"Bingo! I'd much rather have rats nibbling my toes than you jumping off and on my tummy all night long," said Ern at last. "For goodness sake come and lie down."

Tired out at last, Bingo cuddled under the rug and fell asleep. Ern put an arm round him and went to sleep too, dead to the world until morning.

He awoke to hear a stealthy knocking on the door and flew out of bed to open it. Fatty was there – good old Fatty – his pockets bulging. Buster was with him, and immediately went to rub noses with Bingo.

"Hallo, Ern," said Fatty, pushing his way in quickly to prevent the excited Bingo from rushing out. "Got to be a bit careful – Gardener's here this morning, and he'd better not see you in the shed. He might tell Goon!"

"I'll be very careful, then," said Ern, as Fatty pulled a hastily-wrapped packet from one pocket, and some apples from another.

"Here you are, Ern," he said. "Best I could do for the moment. I didn't dare to take too much from the larder, but there were plenty of eggs, so that was something. How's old Bingo? Was he good last night?"

"Well, he seemed to be hunting round for rats for *hours*," said Ern, unwrapping the packet Fatty gave him. "Coo – hard-boiled egg sandwiches – smashing! And two buttered rolls – with honey inside! You're a brick, Fatty, straight you are."

"You'll find some little bottles of lemonade in that cupboard," said Fatty. "And an opener too. I daren't bring you a pot of tea. Mother would start asking questions!"

Ern sat happily munching his egg sandwiches, a glass of lemonade beside him, with Bingo sitting expectantly at his feet. Buster went sniffing at the bottom of a second cupboard, and Fatty laughed.

"He knows a packet of his biscuits is kept there, and he wants to give old Bingo some," said Fatty, getting up. "Am I right, Buster, old thing?"

"Woof!" said Buster, dancing round excitedly, his tail wagging, Bingo joined him, having heard the word biscuits! Soon he and Buster were amiably sharing a packet, crunching up the biscuits in delight.

Buster was overjoyed to have Bingo to play with. He suddenly went completely mad and began to rush round and round the room at top speed, barking wildly. Bingo joined him, and the two boys hurriedly leapt out of the way.

"Shut up, Buster," said Fatty. "Don't do your race-horse gallop in here. Gosh, there goes the lemonade! BUSTER! Have you gone completely mad?"

"BINGO! Oh my goodness, he's got hold of the rug now," said Ern. "He'll tear it to pieces – look at them having a tug-of-war. Fatty, you'll have to take Buster away. They'll wreck everything!"

A cautious knock came at the door and the two dogs left their play and rushed to it, barking madly.

"COME IN!" yelled Fatty. "MIND THE DOGS!"

It was little Bets, come to bring Ern a packet of food. Ern gave her a hug and opened the packet. Bets had made him some potted meat sandwiches, and brought him two currant buns as well. "And next time I come I'll try and bring a pot of jam," she said. "Oh, look at Bingo – he's sitting up and begging! Did you teach him that, Ern?"

"No," said Ern, in surprise. "Perhaps Buster did. Good, Bingo, good! You can stop begging now. Those sandwiches are for *me*."

"I brought Bingo a ball," said Bets feeling in her coat pocket. "Here, Bingo – catch!"

The ball-game became very boisterous, as Buster also joined in, and soon chairs went flying, and rugs slithered

40

about. In the middle of it Fatty's mother looked in at the door.

"Whatever is going on?" she said. "I knocked, Fatty, but there was such a noise I suppose you didn't hear. Why, *Ern* – you here already? You're very early. How is your uncle, Mr. Goon?"

Ern was rather taken-aback. "Ern – well, he has a bit of a cough," he said.

"Dear, dear, I hope he didn't cough all night, poor man," said Mrs. Trotteville.

"I don't know. I didn't hear him coughing at all," said Ern, truthfully.

"You and Bets are here very early today," said Fatty's mother. "Is there a Meeting – or are you going out together, or something?"

"Yes, Mother, yes, we're all going off on an expedition," said Fatty hastily. "We shall be starting pretty soon. Er – any chance of sandwiches for Ern and me?"

"I'll tell Cook," said Mrs. Trotteville, and disappeared up the garden path, much to everyone's relief. Fatty frowned at Buster.

"It was your silly barking, and Bingo's that made Mother come and see what was going on," he said. "Sit! And you too, Bingo – sit – !"

Buster promptly sat, looking up at Fatty with pricked ears. Bingo took one look at him and did the same.

"And now – not another bark out of you, see?" said Fatty to Buster, and Ern pointed his finger at Bingo, and said exactly the same. Bets giggled.

"They look like two naughty little boys – and do look, Bingo is putting his tongue out at you, Ern!"

Sure enough, Bingo's tongue was lolling out of his open mouth, as he sat panting on the rug. His bright eyes were fixed lovingly on Ern.

"Couple of fatheads," said Ern, very proud of his dog. "Now just keep sitting till we say you can get up."

"Look," said Fatty. "I rather think we'd better set off on this first expedition of ours this morning, as I've said we were going. Bets, go and round up Pip and Larry and Daisy, will you? Tell them to be here in half an hour, with bicycles, sandwiches and drinks."

"Right, Fatty," said Bets, happily, and off she went. An expedition all together – to Banshee Towers! It really would be fun.

In just over half an hour everyone was ready. Pip came with Bets, Larry with Daisy, all on their bicycles. Now, how could they get Ern's bicycle too – it was in the shed at Mr. Goon's!

"Uncle will be at the police station by now," said Ern. "I could nip in and get it."

"All right, but for goodness sake don't get caught," said Fatty. Ern shot off, and ran all the way to Mr. Goon's house. He went to the wood-shed, opened it and was thankful to see his bicycle still there. "Good thing Uncle didn't think of it, or he'd have locked it up!" he thought, and rode off at top speed, keeping a wary eye out for Goon. Fortunately he was safely at the police station, very busy indeed.

Soon they were all cycling away down the country lanes, very happy to be going on a picnic to Banshee Hill. The spring sun shone down, the birds sang in the hedges, and the sky was as blue as in summer.

"I can feel some portry coming into my head," said Ern to Bets who was riding beside him.

"Poetry!" said Bets. "Oh, Ern, you're so clever at making up poetry. Do tell it to me! How does it go?"

Ern loved making up what he called his "portry". He went on cycling, his head full of the things he saw around him – primroses in the ditches, cowslips in the fields, new green leaves on the hawthorn, cows grazing, pigeons cooing . . .

"Well, it hasn't quite come yet," he said. "But I know what I'm going to call it – 'Coo'."

"Oh, is it a song the *doves* are going to sing – all about the spring?" said Bets. "Say it to me, Ern."

Ern sailed along on his bicycle, loudly chanting the "portry" that had suddenly come into his head.

"Coo, look at them primroses down in the ditch,
  Smiling all over their faces.
  Coo, listen to all the birds up in the hedge,
  And larks in the big open spaces.
  Coo, look at the cows and the cowslips too,
  And . . . and . . ."

"And what?" said Bets. "Do go on, Ern. It's wonderful."

"Can't seem to think of the end of it," said Ern, frowning. "That's the worst of me when I think of portry, Bets – it comes and goes – and now it's gone. P'raps Fatty can think of the ending."

"We'll ask him when we have our lunch," said Bets. "Look – isn't that Bannshee Hill up there?"

"Coo – what a hill!" said Ern, sounding as if he were beginning his "Coo" song again. "I bet we'll have to walk half way up it. I'll push your bike for you, Bets."

Yes, it was Banshee Hall – a very high one, running up steeply, with a winding road twisting to the summit. As they came near to it, the sun suddenly went in and a great black cloud blew up behind it.

"I suppose that's Banshee Towers right at the very top," said Bets. "Queer-looking place – it stands there as if it's glowering down at us. I don't like it very much – especially with that black cloud behind it."

"You're right,". said Ern, as they began to cycle slowly up the winding road that led to the top. "Very banshee-ish. I should say. Looks as if it wants to grumble and grown and wail! Buck up, young Bets – I believe it's going to pour with rain. Here, let me wheel your bike for you – it's too steep to ride just here!"

Fatty had just turned round to see if the girls were managing all right, and was pleased to see Ern wheeling Bets' bicycle for her. Ern might be rough and ready sometimes, but he had very nice ways, thought Fatty. He called to Daisy.

"Want any help, Daisy?"

"No, I'm all right," said Daisy, panting. "I just hope we'll get to the top before it pours! I say – that looks a pretty grim place up on the hill, doesn't it?"

"Yes – more like an old fortress than anything!" shouted back Fatty. "Look at the two dogs – we've left them far behind! Never mind – they'll catch us up some-time."

They arrived at the gloomy old place at last, and stacked their bicycles in a convenient shed. Then they made their way to the entrance.

"This way to the Wailing Banshee!" said Larry, grinning at Daisy and Bets. "Make ready to run for your lives!"

"Ass!" said Fatty, seeing Bets' alarmed face. "I'll make you run for your life if you say any more, Larry! Come on – we have to pay to go in so dub up!'

Inside Banshee Towers

"How much to go in, please?" asked Fatty.

"One shilling each," said the dour-looking man behind the turnstiles.

"Whew – that's rather a lot for us children to pay," said Pip. "Don't we go in for half-price?"

44

"You do not," said the man, looking at them severely over the top of his spectacles.

"Do you charge for dogs?" asked Fatty.

"No. They are NOT allowed in here," said the man. "Anyway, you haven't any dogs with you."

"We seem to have lost them," said Fatty. "Er – do you charge for cats? I can see one sitting in your office."

"And what about horses?" said Larry, joining in. "Any objection to horses or a sheep or two?"

"No horses and no sheep," said the man. "And no silly asses, either, so be careful if *you* want to go in, see?"

"He's smarter than he looks," said Fatty to the others when they were safely inside. "Let's buy a catalogue shall we? I say – what a place!"

"And what a VIEW!" said Daisy, going to one of the great windows that looked down over the countryside. "Glorious! You can see everything for miles around!"

"Fatty! Come and look at this picture!" called Bets. "It's so real you can almost hear the swish of the waves!"

They all went across the stone floor, their feet clattering, to a wall where a great picture was displayed – a stormy sea, the waves rising high, the spray flying.

"I feel as if my face is getting wet with spray when I look at that," said Bets, in awe. "Isn't it magnificent! Do buy a catalogue, Fatty. I want to see what it says about this picture."

Fatty went back to the man at the turnstiles, took a catalogue and put down a shilling, the man didn't even look up. "Surly fellow!" thought Fatty and went back to the others, leafing through the catalogue to find a description of the picture that Bets liked.

"It's called 'Fury of the Storm'," he said. "It says the artist is one of the most famous of sea-artists – and would you believe it, that picture was painted more than a hundred years ago! And yet it looks as fresh and clear as if it had been finished yesterday."

Someone clattered over the stone-floor, set down a stool and put an easel in front of a picture on the opposite wall. He proceeded to set up a large canvas on the easel. The children went over, in curiosity.

"Hallo, kids," said the man, a shock-haired fellow in a loose black painting overall. "Come to worship at the shrine of sea-art? Mind you don't bump into the banshee. It wails one day a week, you know, so you *may* hear it."

"I don't want to," said Bets, at once. "Anyway, there isn't a banshee, it's just imaginary."

There was further clattering, and three more artists came in, carrying easels. They set themselves down in front of various pictures. Fatty stared in surprise.

"Are you *copying* the pictures?" he asked the man beside him, who was now sitting on a stool, mixing colours on a palette.

"Yes. We all belong to a School of Art," said the man. "Those who are good enough are sent here to copy these pictures for practice – we can sell them all right afterwards, you know."

Bets looked at the picture on the man's easel. It didn't seem very good to her. "You haven't painted that wave the right colour," she said, pointing.

"Well, alter it for me," said the man, offering her an enormously long paint-brush.

"Oh, I couldn't," said Bets.

"See that fellow over there?" said the man, pointing with his brush. "Well, he's the best of the lot. He doesn't belong to our art-school, though. You go and see *his* work – better than the original artist's, I sometimes think!"

They went over to look at the picture the other man was copying. He sat in front of a lovely seascape, that

46

shone on the wall opposite the man. It was a picture of a blue sea swirling round the bottom of a high cliff, tumbling over the rocks. On his big canvas he was reproducing a marvellous copy. He scowled at the children.

"*Allez vous en!*" he growled.

"That's French for 'Go away'," Bets whispered to the surprised Ern. "We'd better go."

But Ern wouldn't move. He stood staring at the picture on the wall, his face full of wonder and awe. To think anyone could paint the sea like that – why, it was *real* – you could almost hear the wind and the roar of the waves – you could feel the spray and . . .

"Wake up, Ern," said Larry. "You'll shout for a lifeboat if you look at that picture any more!"

"It's smashing," said Ern. "Ab-so-lutely smashing. Wish *I* could paint. Gosh, if I'd painted that picture there, I'd never do anything but sit and look at it all day long!"

The French artist who was copying the picture suddenly lost his temper as Ern breathed heavily down the back of his neck. He leapt up, drew his paint-brush across Ern's face, and hissed at him with a long string of what sounded like complete gibberish to the startled Ern.

"Come on, we've upset the fellow," said Fatty, seeing the alarm on Bets' face. "Sorry, sir – but you shouldn't lash out with your brush like that. Ern, come with me. ERN!"

But Ern was still staring at the picture on the wall, absent-mindedly rubbing at the paint that the artist had streaked across his face. Larry chuckled. Ern looked rather like a clown now! Fatty and Larry took him firmly by the arms and led him to the opposite side of the great hall, where other pictures were.

Ern and Bets could have stayed there all day,

47

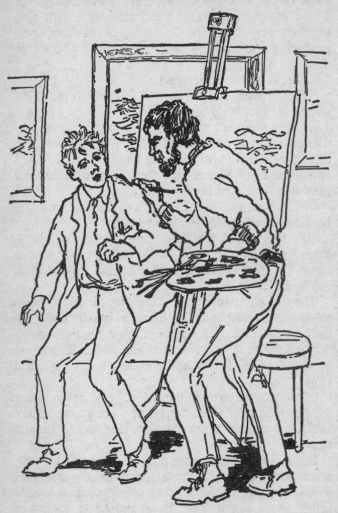

He leapt up and drew his paintbrush across Ern's face.

staring at the pictures. There seemed to be some magic about the seascapes that appealed to each of them in a way that the others did not feel. Soon they left Bets and Ern to themselves and wandered into the other rooms. Here there was old armour on the walls, and old weapons in cases. The four examined them with much interest, and Fatty longed to take down a great old pike from the wall, and caper about with it.

"I don't see why we shouldn't have our picnic in *here*, do you?" said Larry, looking out of one of the great windows. "That enormous black cloud is now pouring down sheets of rain. We can't picnic out-of-doors. We needn't make any mess at all, and we'll take all our litter home with us."

"I bet that bad-tempered fellow out at the turnstile won't let us stay," said Fatty.

"What's it to do with *him*?" said Larry. "We've paid, haven't we? Anyway, I'm jolly hungry. Gosh, was that thunder?"

It was! The children felt all the more determined to stay in Banshee Towers for shelter, and have their lunch there. Ern was longing to – not because of the lunch, but because of the pictures. He simply could not take his eyes off them!

The six sat down in a corner of one of the great rooms, behind a kind of large settee. Now if that turn-stile man looked in, he wouldn't see them and turn them out!

"Wonder where the dogs are?" said Fatty, suddenly. "They ought to have been here long ago."

"Gone rabbiting halfway up the hill, I expect," said Ern. "Or else that turnstile man wouldn't let them in! They'll be all right. They'll either turn up – or go home!"

"Some of those artists are leaving," said Larry. "I can hear them packing up and shouting goodbye. Hallo,

49

who are these? Peep through the arms of the settee, Fatty – visitors, do you think?"

Yes – they certainly looked like sightseers. There were three women and a man, and they ambled aimlessly round, looking at the pictures and the old armour.

"Not worth a shilling, to come in and see all this junk – and I never did like sea-pictures," said one woman. "All those picture waves that never break, but just rear up and keep still! Gives me the willies!"

To the children's dismay, the visitors sat down on the settee behind which they were hiding, and began to rustle paper, unpacking their lunch. "All them silly tales too, about banshees wailing!" said the man. "We've wasted our shillings. It would be *worth* a shilling to hear a banshee wail – but *there*, I never did believe in things like that."

It was at this moment that Fatty suddenly felt impelled to be a banshee. The idea came to him in a flash, and he couldn't stop himself. He opened his mouth and let out a marvellous wail, eerie, long-drawn, high-pitched and really terrifying!

"Eeee-ooooo-ohhhhh-eeee-oh-oooOOOOO-OO!"

The man and the three women leapt up from the settee as if they had rockets under them. One of the women screamed, and then they all four fled at top speed to the door and out into the great hall to the entrance where the turnstiles stood.

Not only the visitors jumped almost out of their skin. Larry, Daisy, Pip, Bets and Ern jumped too, and clutched in fright at one another, when the eerie wail echoed round them. Larry realized almost at once that it was Fatty, and he gave him a very hard punch.

"Fathead! What did you do that for? I almost died of fright! Look at poor Bets – she's trembling!"

Fatty, overcome with laughter and shame at one and

the same time, couldn't say a word. Gradually the others joined him in laughter, and the six of them rolled about, trying not to laugh too loudly.

"Oh, their faces!" groaned Fatty. "Oh, what made me do it? I'm awfully sorry but it just sort of came over me. Oh, how they skedaddled! And *your* faces too! Oh, I *must* laugh again, and I've such a stitch in my side!"

"I bet any artists left skedaddled too!" said Pip, wiping his eyes. "You're a horror, Fatty. The things you think of! Honestly, if it had been a real banshee wailing, it couldn't have done it better. I do think . . ."

But what he thought the others never knew, because a most extraordinary noise gradually began to echo all around – high-pitched, wailing, unhappy! It went on and on, and Bets and Daisy clutched at the boys in real terror.

"Fatty – that's *not* you this time, is it, Fatty?" said Daisy, in a shaking voice. "Oh, what is it? I don't like it, I don't. I don't. Tell it to stop."

But the wailing went on and on, mournful and miserable, and soon the children huddled together in fear, amazed and frightened.

At last it stopped, and they all heaved a sigh of relief. "Let's get out of here," said Larry. "It's all right, Bets. It was probably just a silly echo wailing round the hill. Cheer up! Fatty, bring the lunch – we'll have it somewhere else. DO come on!"

A strange discovery!

Fatty collected the lunch and they all crept out from behind the large old settee. They walked with rather shaky legs across the room to the great hall where the artists had sat, copying the pictures. Now only one was left – the Frenchman who had been copying the picture that Ern had liked so much.

He was rolling up a canvas very carefully, whistling below his breath. He jumped when he saw the children coming in, and looked annoyed.

"So you have no fear of the banshee?" he said. "You are brave, brave, brave! See, all the others have gone. *Ils avaient peur* – they were so, so afraid. But I – I am not afraid of the banshees – nor of – how do you call it – goosts?"

"Ghosts," said Fatty. "Do you *really* mean to say you weren't scared?"

"No – but today there was something – something – how do you say it – queer? First there was *one* banshee wailing – and then, there was a *second*. I suppose, *mes enfants,* you know nothing of the *first* banshee?"

Fatty felt himself going red, but he wasn't going to admit anything to this laughing man. He didn't like him very much.

"Are you going?" asked Fatty, seeing the man tying the canvas he had been rolling up.

"Just to the village to my car – and then back again to paint, paint, paint!" said the man, and dug Fatty in the chest with his roll of canvas. "And you – you stay here to wail, wail, wail? Ah, what a naughty boy!"

And taking no notice of Fatty's angry face, he strolled across the hall and vaulted over the turnstiles as easily as an acrobat.

"I suppose he thinks he's very clever," growled Fatty, not at all enjoying being laughed at by the artist.

"Listen, it's still pouring with rain. We can't picnic on the hills, we'll have to have it here, banshee or no banshee. Don't look so scared, Bets – a wailing can't hurt us."

"The turnstile fellow has gone," said Larry, looking across to where the man had sat when he took their money: "Gone to *his* lunch, I suppose. Well, we should be pretty safe in this hall. Come on – let's eat something. We'll feel better then!"

So they went over to where a great wooden seat stood, beside an old oak table. Fatty unpacked the lunch, and soon they were all sitting down, eating it, surprised to find that they were so hungry after their fright.

"Ern, tell Fatty your poem," said Bets, suddenly, seeing a piece of paper sticking out of Ern's pocket, and feeling certain that Ern had managed to find time to write down his "pome".

"Poem?" said Fatty, surprised. "Have you been going in for poetry again, Ern?"

"Er – well, Fatty, it's only a silly sort of pome – I mean poem," said Ern, blushing. "I've called it 'Coo'."

"Ah, it's about doves or pigeons then, is it?" said Fatty. "Cooing."

"Well, not *exactly* that sort of coo," sad Ern, anxiously. "It's reely the sort of 'coo' you say when you're surprised, like. I've got it written down here. I must say I feel like writing a pome about the sea too, now, after seeing all those sea-pictures."

"You're a wonder, Ern," said Fatty, and meant it. "Come along, where's this poem?"

"I couldn't *finish it*, Fatty," said Ern, looking at it.

"That's the worst of me. It all comes in a rush, like, and then fades out and I can't think of a good ending."

"Well, read it Ern," said Fatty. So Ern, blushing again, read out his "pome", at top speed.

"Coo, look at them primroses down in the ditch,
Smiling all over their faces.
Coo, listen to all the birds up in the hedge,
And larks in the big open spaces.
Coo, look at the cows and the cowslips too,
And . . ."

Ern stopped and looked pleadingly at Fatty. "I can't think of the end, Fatty. I just can't."

"Oh *yes*, Ern – there's only one *possible* ending," said Fatty, and carried on at once.

"Coo, look at the cows and the cowslips too,
And the lions so dandy and yellow,
And the cups full of butter for me and for you,
And hark where the bulrushes bellow!
Coo, look at the runner beans, how fast they go,
And . . ."

By this time the others were laughing so much that Fatty had to stop for breath and laugh too. Ern stared at him in admiration. "How do you do it, Fatty?" he asked, solemnly. "Takes me ages to think of even one line, and you just go rattling on and on – coo, I'd never have thought of that line, 'Look at the runner beans, how fast they go!' That's right down funny, Fatty."

"Dear old Ern, your lines are poetry, and mine are not," said Fatty, clapping him on the back. "Yours are just a bit too 'cooey' that's all. 'Coo' isn't a good word for poetry, unless it's said by a dove!"

"You're a wonder, you are," said Ern, remembering

another of Fatty's lines. "Lions so dandy and yellow – you meant the yellow dandelions there didn't you – honest, Fatty, you're a genius."

"Let's change the subject," said Fatty, feeling rather a fraud. He could reel off verse without stopping, ridiculous, amusing and clever, and could never think why everyone thought it wonderful.

"Everybody finished?" asked Larry, screwing up his papers. "There's a litter basket over there."

"I say," said Pip, suddenly. "What do you suppose has happened to Buster and Bingo? They ought to be here by now, surely?"

"Oh, I expect they turned tail and went home when they got too far behind," said Fatty. "They probably lost our trail. We shan't see them till we get home. I only hope they are behaving themselves."

A sudden, very familiar noise made them all jump! "Woof! WOOF!"

"Golly – *that* sounds like them!" said Ern in amazement. "Where are they? I can't see them anywhere!"

"Wuff – woof!"

"They're both about somewhere!" said Fatty, puzzled. "But their barks sound a bit muffled. BUSTER! BINGO! Where on earth are you?"

A scrabbling noise came from the big fireplace and the children went over to it at once. An old iron cauldron stood squarely in the middle of the wide hearth, and the barking seemed to come from under there. Fatty lifted up the heavy old thing, and gave a loud exclamation.

"OHO! What have we here? Look – a neat, round trap-door! The dogs seem to be under it somewhere. Bets, go and see if there's anyone about whose permission we can ask to pull up the trap-door."

Bets ran to the turnstile and looked all about. There was no one to be seen. She hurried back.

"No, Fatty, I can't see a soul. I expect the turnstile man is away having his dinner – and the artists haven't come back yet, though they've left their easels here."

"Right. Then we'll have to yank up the trap-door *without* permission!" said Fatty. "Help me, Ern."

There was now such a loud and excited barking coming from beneath the trap-door that it seemed almost as if there might be half a dozen dogs below, not just two!

"How *did* they get there?" said Larry, watching Fatty and Ern heaving up the trap-door. "They can't possibly have got down through the trap-door – so they must have found a way into the hill – and gone up an underground tunnel to Banshee Towers."

"Oooh – a Secret Passage!" said Bets, her eyes shining. "Can we go down it?"

"Here she comes!" said Fatty, panting hard as he and Ern heaved the trap-door out of its place. Immediately the two dogs hurled themselves out, and fell upon Ern and Fatty in rhapsodies of joy, barking, licking, pawing as if they had gone mad.

"Steady on, steady on," said Fatty, pushing Buster down. "Buster, will you kindly tell me how you got here?"

"Woof!" said Buster, dancing about happily.

"And how did *you* get here, Bingo," demanded Ern, whose dog seemed intent on licking every single inch of his face. "Stop it, Bingo. I shall have to borrow a towel from somewhere soon. Keep your tongue in your mouth for a bit. Oh, goodness, there he goes again!"

Larry was looking down the hole where the trap-door had been. He took out a small torch from his pocket and switched it on. He gave a sudden exclamation.

"Look – there are steps cut down from the hearth – almost like ladder steps, going down and down. Where on *earth* do they go to?"

"We might have time to explore a bit," said Fatty, feeling thrilled to see the steps leading down into the darkness. "Bets – go and see if we're still the only ones here."

Bets ran off and then came back, her face rather frightened. "Fatty, the turnstile man is coming up the hill. He's nearly here. Put the trap-door back, quickly!"

Ern and Fatty lifted the trap-door into place and then put the heavy cauldron over it. They were still kneeling down by the fireplace when the turnstile man came in, munching an apple. He gave an angry shout when he saw them.

"Quick – pretend we've dropped a shilling," said Fatty, in a low, urgent voice. "Look for it, all of you – in the hearth and on the carpet too – quick!"

So, when the puzzled turnstile man ran up, they were all apparently hunting feverishly for a lost shilling!

"*Must* find it!" Fatty was saying. "Simply must. A shilling is a shilling. Where on earth did it go? Is that it over there, Bets?"

"Oh, so you've dropped some money, have you?" said the man. "Sure that's all you're up to? Let *me* have a look!" And down he dropped on hands and knees too. He gave a sudden shout, and picked something up.

"I've got it. Here it is!" And he held up a shilling in triumph.

"Thanks," said Fatty, and held out his hand. But the man laughed in his face, and slipped the coin into his trouser pocket, "Finding's keeping," he said. "Now you go off, all of you. You've been here long enough. And how did those dogs get in? You ought to pay for them, you did."

"Oh, aren't they *your* dogs?" said Ern, in such a surprised voice that Bets had to put her hand over her mouth to stop a laugh escaping.

"*My* dogs! I should think not. I can't bear them!"

said the man, and made as if he were going to kick Buster. Buster growled and showed his teeth and the man backed hurriedly away. "Go on, now – you clear out," he said. "Thursday's my afternoon off, and I want a bit of peace!"

And, very thankfully, the children did clear out, and went to fetch their bicycles, the dogs gambolling round.

"What a bit of luck a shilling had been dropped in that hearth sometime, by somebody," said Ern, as they all mounted.

"Dear Ern – I dropped it there *myself*," grinned Fatty. "I knew if that fellow found it, as I meant him to, he wouldn't worry about the trap-door any more! Come on now, home, everyone. Home, Buster! Bingo! HOME!"

Home again – and a good long talk

"Well – that was a rather surprising expedition!" said Fatty, when they were well away from Banshee Towers. "I feel we have quite a lot to think about. The wailing of the banshee – I don't mean *my* wailing, of course, that wasn't a patch on the old banshee's – my word, *she* could wail all right!"

"Don't remind me of it," said Bets, with a shudder. "I just want to put Banshee Towers behind me and ride away home down this hill, as quickly as I can!"

"And then there was that queer trap-door in the hearth," said Larry. "And the puzzle of how on earth the dogs arrived underneath it."

"And *I* didn't like the look of that turnstile man at all," announced Daisy. "I thought he looked a villain."

"Oh, not as bad as *that*," said Pip. "He just looked

bored and bad-tempered – and I must say I would too, if I had a turnstile job on the top of a cold hill in a place where banshees wailed!"

"I'd like to get home and talk about it," said Larry. "I don't know what *you* think, Fatty, but it all seems pretty queer to me."

"A bit of a mystery, you mean?" said Fatty. "Well – it's about time that the Five Find-Outers had a good juicy mystery to solve, isn't it?"

"Oh *yes*!" said Pip, in delight. "We've never had one with banshees in before."

"Well, I could do without banshees, really," said Bets. "What about telling the Chief Inspector – you know, Inspector Jenks – he might . . ."

"Bets, we really *can't* tell him silly stories of banshees," said Fatty. "They don't *really* exist, you know. They . . ."

"All right – well, what *was* it that we heard this afternoon?" said Bets. "I don't care what its name is, it was as bad and weird and horrible as any banshee, so there!"

"You're right, Bets. It was pretty awful," said Pip. "I didn't like it myself. Real or unreal, that banshee is MOST mysterious. Look out, now, we're coming to a very steep bit. Go as slowly as you can all the way, in case your brakes are weak."

Away down the hill they sailed in a long line, the the two dogs galloping manfully – or "dogfully" as Bets said – after them. What a day they had had – and how they all longed to be down in Fatty's workroom and talk about it – and make plans to solve yet another Mystery! Bets shivered with excitement. There always seemed to be a mystery of some sort when Fatty was around!

Everyone was glad to be in Fatty's cosy workroom, especially the two dogs, who were quite tired out with their long run. Buster flopped down in his basket, panting, and Bingo fell on top of him, too tired to play. In half a second they were sound asleep.

"One great basketful of dogs," said Bets, smiling. "I'm glad they're such friends."

"It's nice for Bingo to have a friend like Buster – you know, well-brought-up, like," said Ern. "I want Bingo to have good manners. He'll learn from old Buster – real copy-cat Bingo is!"

"No, no," said Fatty, gravely. "There you make a mistake, Ern. Not a copy-cat, surely – a copy-*dog*!

"Ha ha – funny joke," said Pip, who was tired, and not in the mood for Fatty's quips.

"I'm thirsty," said Larry. "Any orange squash Fatty?"

"Plenty in my cupboard," said Fatty. "And glasses too. And there's some chocolate somewhere. Buck up and get what you want. I'm longing to discuss the strange happenings of this morning. You know – I think Something's Going On Up There."

"Up where?" asked Ern.

"Banshee Hill, ass," said Fatty. "Two things puzzle me – that banshee wail – and the hole under the hearth, where that cauldron stands."

"Well, what's puzzling about the banshee wail?" asked Bets. "You *said* that's what banshees did – wail and howl and cry."

"Yes – but you heard what that artist in the black overall said," went on Fatty. "He said that the banshee only wailed one day a week! Well – why only *one* day?"

"Perhaps banshees only *do* wail one day a week." suggested Daisy. "I mean – all that awful wailing must be a terrible strain on the throat. I bet *your* throat felt sore after you'd wailed at the top of your voice – you sound a bit husky to me."

"Well, I'm *not*, said Fatty. "I could wail like that for half an hour or more and not feel husky."

"For goodness sake don't do anything of the sort," said Larry. "You'd have the fire-brigade here and the police, and every doctor in the place."

"Do come back to the point, Larry." said Fatty. "WHY does the banshee only wail once a week? There can't be a real banshee there – there aren't such things. It must be somebody faking one – but why?"

"For fun," said Bets.

"Yes, but why on a certain *day*?" persisted Fatty.

"What on earth does it matter?" said Pip, getting tired of the subject. "It can wail *every* day of the week, for all I care."

"Pip, you should have a more alert, enquiring mind," said Fatty, solemnly. "You know – that's a fake banshee – and I'd jolly well like to find out who's working it and how – and why."

"I don't want to go up that hill again," said Bets. "I loved the pictures – but I hated the wailing."

"Don't worry, Bets. You needn't go. But *I'm* going," said Fatty. "I'm going tomorrow. I tell you, I Smell a Mystery!"

"Well, you must have the most powerful nose anybody ever had," said Larry. "All I can smell is that oil-stove smoking. I suppose your nose is too high and mighty to smell ordinary things like that. Turn down the wick, Ern – you're nearest."

Ern turned down the wick carefully. "Fatty," he said, "could I come with you if you go to Banshee Hill tomorrow – not to mess about in a mystery, though – just to see those sea-pictures again. Especially the one with the high cliffs and the blue sea swirling round it."

"Oh – the one the French artist was copying," said Fatty. "Yes, that was a beauty. All right, Ern, you can come with me – you'll be company – and while you stand and gloat over the pictures, I can do a little snooping. It's just as well I should have someone with me who is obviously there to see the pictures!"

"Oooh, thanks, Fatty," said Ern, "I hope that banshee doesn't come wailing round me, though."

"It only wails *once* a week, Ern," said Fatty. "I'll eat my cap if it wails tomorrow! I'm pretty certain it has its pet day, for *some* reason or other."

"Look – we'd better go, Daisy and I," said Larry, getting up in a hurry. "Gosh – I'd quite forgotten our Granny was coming to tea. Buck up, Daisy, for goodness sake. We're going out for the day tomorrow, Fatty, so we won't be seeing you. So long!"

They shot out of the shed door and the others heard them racing up the garden. Pip stood up then, and yanked Bets to her feet. "Come along, Bets," he said. "You look half asleep. Telephone us, Fatty, when there's a Meeting again."

"I should think Bets is tired out with the long bicycle ride," said Fatty, giving Bets a hug. "Goodbye, Bets – and don't dream of banshees tonight!"

"I hope I'm not being a nuisance to you, Fatty," said Ern, when the others had gone. "Staying here in your shed."

"No – no, of *course* you're not a nuisance, Ern," said Fatty. "Hallo – who's this coming – I seem to know those heavy footsteps."

"It's Uncle!" said Ern, in alarm. "He must have heard that I've not gone home. Fatty, hide me!"

"There's nowhere to hide you," said Fatty, looking round. "He'd look in that cupboard at once! Listen now, Ern, I'll lock the door – and when your uncle comes knocking on it, you slip quietly out of the window, see? I'll hand Bingo to you. Hide somewhere and come back when Goon is gone."

62

Bang-bang-bang! That was Goon at the shed door. Fatty had quickly turned the key in the lock, so the policeman could not open it. A roar came from the other side.

"Frederick Trotteville, you open this door. I know you've got Ern in there. I saw him through the window. You open this door or I'll go to your father."

"*Ern?* Ern in *here*, Mr Goon! You must be seeing things!" shouted Fatty, going to the door. "Wait a minute – it's locked. Shut up, Buster, making that row!"

Buster and Bingo were certainly making a terrific noise. Neither of them liked Mr. Goon, and they had recognized his voice at once. Ern was now getting out of the window at the side of the shed. He patted the sill and Bingo came running to him, and leapt into his arms. "Sh!" said Ern. "No barking, now." He crept off to where a thick clump of bushes grew, and squeezed into the middle of them.

Fatty quietly shut the window after him and ran back to the door, on which Goon was still angrily hammering. "Be patient, Mr Goon," said Fatty. "The key seems to have stuck – ah – it's all right now – there we are!"

He turned the key smartly, and flung open the door. The angry policeman stormed into the shed at once, shouting at the top of his voice "Ern! ERN! You come alonga me. You never went home! You disobeyed me! You just wait and see what . . ."

But Goon didn't finish what he had to say because Buster flung himself on him with enormous delight, trying to nip his ankles through the thick trousers.

"GAH!" said Mr Goon, kicking out. "That dog again! Where's Ern? I saw him, I know I did!"

"Well, have a good look round, Mr. Goon," said

Ern was getting out of the window at the side of the shed.

Fatty, politely. "He may be under that stool – or behind the books in the bookcase – or in the dog's basket. Buster, stop that row."

Goon was quite at a loss as he stood staring round the room. He *had* seen Ern there, he knew he had. It didn't occur to him that Ern had had time to slip out of the window. He glared at Fatty, and glared at Buster, and turned to go. Buster gave a blood-curdling growl, and Goon shot out of the door at top speed.

"You wait!" he shouted, as Fatty shut the door. "I'll get Ern all right – ho yes, I'll get him!" And away he went, muttering to himself. "That toad of a boy – too clever by half, he is. Where *is* Ern? Just wait till I get hold of him. He won't sit down properly for a week, that he won't!"

Banshee Towers again

When the policeman had gone, Ern crept out of the middle of the bush, and went back to Fatty's shed, grinning. "Thanks, Fatty," he said. "You're a pal! I say – you're sure you don't mind if I go up to Banshee Towers with you tomorrow?"

"Be nice to have your company, Ern," said Fatty, and meant it! "Also, you may be useful. You see – I do want to snoop around a bit, and if there are people there, you might be able to take up their attention somehow . . . so that no one will be watching *me*."

"But how do I take up anyone's attention?" said Ern. alarmed. "I'm no good at play-acting, Fatty, you know that."

"Oh, Ern, you can do a sudden bit of tap dancing – or sing a little song – or pretend to faint," said Fatty.

"I'll signal to you like this, if I want you to turn people's attention to you, and away from me!"

And Fatty smoothed back his hair three times. "See? Don't look so alarmed. Nobody will lock you up, or box your ears. They'll just stay still in astonishment, and forget all about me and what I'm doing."

"All right, Fatty," said Ern, in a mournful voice, and settled down to read one of Fatty's books. "Coo, the books you've got, Fatty – you must have over a thousand. This one's smashing."

He was soon lost in the sea-story he had found in Fatty's big bookcase. Bingo lay happily on Ern's feet, and Buster sat as close to Fatty as he could. Ern came to the end of a chapter, and looked up in great content. He was perfectly happy. He had a friend, a dog, a good book, and somewhere quiet to read. Ern gave an enormous sigh and went back to his book, thinking how lucky he was to have a clever friend like Fatty.

Next morning Ern woke up feeling excited. He sat up on the camp-bed in the shed trying to remember the reason for his excitement. "Of course – Fatty and I are going up to that Banshee place again – and I shall see those grand pictures," he thought, in delight. "Bingo – do you hear that? Sh, don't bark too loudly. Nobody must know we're here. I've told you that before."

Bingo had snuggled down on Ern's feet all night long. He sat up, yawning, wondering when his friend Buster would come. Bingo thought the world of Buster, and copied him in every way he could, even to rubbing his nose with his left paw, instead of his right one. He crawled over Ern's knees and gave him a smacking lick on the nose. Then he rolled over to be tickled.

"Do you know something, Bingo?" said Ern, solemnly. "Right now I am feeling very very sorry for all those boys and girls who haven't a dog of their own. They just don't know what they're missing. Now then –

that's enough licking. Go and fetch me that towel, so that I can wipe my face. Good dog, then – clever dog! You understand everything I say, don't you? Now, please take the towel back. Jolly good, Bingo!"

Fatty brought Ern some breakfast, and then disappeared to do a few jobs for his mother. "I'll be back at ten and we'll set off," he said. "We'll take lunch with us – I'll buy it on the way, because Cook is getting a bit suspicious of the enormous appetite I seem suddenly to have developed. She said this morning that I seem to want enough for *two* people – and she was right!"

They set off just after ten, and Fatty stopped to buy some sandwiches, new currant buns, and oranges. He had already put some lemonade and a cup into his bicycle basket. Ern gave a sudden cry of alarm, as they rode up the village street.

"Fatty – there's my uncle!"

Sure enough, there was Mr. Goon, standing at the cross-roads, directing the busy traffic with a frown. He couldn't believe his eyes when he saw Ern cycling along with Fatty! Stop!" he bawled. "Ern! You heard me. STOP!"

But alas, Ern disobeyed the Law, and pedalled faster than ever, leaving poor Mr. Goon very angry indeed!

"Woof!" said a loud voice, as they pedalled past Mr. Goon – and Buster suddenly stuck his head out of a wooden box that Fatty had tied to his rear mudguard! Bingo was in a similar box, on the back of Ern's bicycle, but he was so much afraid of Mr. Goon that he didn't dare to venture even the smallest bark, as he passed him. He didn't want to be plucked away from his beloved Ern by the loud-voiced Mr. Goon!

"Good idea to take the dogs with us this way," said Ern. "I reckon it's really too far for them to run all the way there and back. They seem to like the ride, don't they, Fatty? Gosh, *I'm* enjoying it too."

As soon as they were out of the town, Fatty burst into song.

> *"Up the street*
> *On pedalling feet,*
> *Here we go, Ern and I!*
> *And a song we sing*
> *With a ting-a-ling-ling,*
> *As we both go bicycling by!*
> *Our wheels go round*
> *With a swishity sound,*
> *As fast as the wind we fly,*
> *Through village and town,*
> *Now up, now down,*
> *Here we go, Ern and I!*

Ern almost fell off his bicycle in admiration. "Coo, Fatty – did you just make that up this very minute – just like that?"

"It suddenly came into my head," said Fatty, modestly. "It goes nicely with our pedalling, Ern, doesn't it?" And the two of them sang the Bicycling Song, as Ern called it, at the tops of their voices, pedalling in strict time to the rhythm of the lines!

Buster didn't like the singing, and began to bark. Fatty turned round and addressed him. "No, Buster – you've got the words wrong – *and* the tune as well."

That made Ern laugh. They pedalled on happily and soon came to the steep hill, up which they had to toil slowly. Banshee Towers glowered at the top as if not welcoming them at all. When they arrived there, the boys put their bicycles into the racks provided in the shed, and sauntered to the turnstile. Buster and Bingo running at their heels.

"Oh – you again," said the man, grumpily. "Plus dogs! Didn't I say that *no* dogs were allowed? I'd just like to know how those dogs got into Banshee Towers yesterday."

"I've no idea," said Fatty. "They suddenly appeared. One minute they were not there. The next they were. No one was more surprised than *we* were."

"They can stay in that shed over there," said the man. "But they can't go indoors. See?"

"Right," said Fatty, paying out two shillings. "I say, tell me one thing – does the old banshee wail on one special day each week – and if so, why?"

"The legend says that it was on a Thursday that calamity came to the Lord of Banshee Towers," said the man. "And so the banshee wails that same day."

"Oh – so Thursday is always the banshee's great day?" said Fatty. "Very interesting. Have you any idea where your banshee lives?"

"Don't ask daft questions," said the turnstile man, losing his temper. "Go on in and don't come bothering me."

"Just *one* more question," said Fatty. "Tell me – when did the banshee first begin to wail in modern times? It says in the catalogue that she used to wail a hundred years ago – or so the legend went – but hadn't been known to wail since. I saw that the catalogue was printed six years ago. What made the banshee begin to wail again – did she conveniently find her voice six years ago, when the catalogue was printed, and this place was thrown open to the public?"

"Are you trying to say that the banshee isn't real – that she's a fraud?" said the man, angrily. "Well, you ask the tall, dark man you'll see in the Armour Room today – *he'll* soon put you right. He owns this place, see – and *he* ought to know about the banshee, didn't he?"

"Ah, now that's information worth having," said Fatty, looking pleased. "I'll certainly have a chat with the man who owns the place *and* the banshee too. Thanks a lot. What's his name?"

"He's an Austrian," said the man, still very cross. "Name of Engler. And I hope he wipes the floor with you, you fat nuisance!"

"Now, now!" said Fatty, raising a finger in reproof, just as if he were a nurse addressing a child. "Now, now – mustn't be rude. Mustn't lose tempers! Don't want to put you into a corner!"

And with that Fatty marched off to put the dogs into the shed, leaving a most irritated man behind him, and accompanied by a rather scared but most admiring Ern.

"I don't know how you can hold your own like that, Fatty," he said. "Straight I don't. Look – there's the Frenchman we saw yesterday. Wonder how he's got on with the picture he was copying."

"*Bonjour*," said Fatty politely to the Frenchman, who was hurrying down the great hall, carrying a rolled-up canvas. "Finished your picture?"

"Ah, *bonjour, mon ami!*" said the Frenchman. "You come back so soon?"

"Well, my friend here loves the sea-pictures," said Fatty. "You see, he wants to go into the Navy, so anything to do with the sea attracts him, even if it's only pictures. Won't you show us the copy you made of that grand picture? Is that it you are carrying?"

"Yes, yes, but I must hurry, or I would show it to you," said the Frenchman, giving a polite little bow. "Someone awaits me outside. *Au revoir!* We shall meet again if you come often to this place. I am always here!"

He scurried off. Fatty looked after him thoughtfully. Funny little man! He looked round for the owner of the place, the Austrian called – what was it now – oh yes, Engler. That must be the man over there, in the Armour Room. Tall. Dark. Foreign-looking. He looked a hard sort of man. Better be careful of him!

"You go and have a look at your magnificent sea-picture, Ern," said Fatty. "I'll go and talk to the Austrian owner. I want to ask him a few questions about banshees."

"Right," said Ern, and wandered off happily round the big room, looking at this picture and that, saving his favourite picture to the last.

He came to it eventually, and stood in front of it, gazing at the great high cliff, the swirling waves, the grim rocks. He stared at the sea-gulls tossed by the tempestuous wind, and imagined himself in a boat on that angry sea, swept by foaming waves, the wind howling in his ears. Ha – if only *he* could paint a picture like that! It would be almost better than going into the Navy. No – on second thoughts he'd rather go to sea.

Ern stood for some time opposite the picture. Then suddenly a puzzled look came over his face. He stood closer to the picture and peered at the sea from this side and that. He scratched his head. He stood further back. Then he went to one side and stood there, and then to the other side, screwing up his eyes as if he were trying to see something. He shook his head and frowned.

"I'll have to find Fatty," he said at last. "It's a puzzle, this is. Can't make it out! Where *is* Fatty? Oh, there he is, talking to that man, Fatty! FATTY! Here, I've got something to ask you!"

Ern's queer discovery

Fatty had studied the Austrian owner of Banshee Towers, and had decided that he didn't look to be the type that usually bought old places just because they were beautiful! "He's a sharp business man, if I ever saw one!" thought Fatty. "It beats me why he bought this out-of-the-way place. He can't make much money out of visitors, except for a month or two in the summer. I wonder if he owns the pictures as well."

The Austrian was sitting on the big settee behind which the children had hidden the day before. He was studying a catalogue of some sort, frowning over it. He was big and burly, with great eyebrows and a big nose.

Fatty went up to him, and spoke in his politest voice. "Excuse me, sir, for interrupting – but I believe you own this magnificent old place?"

"What – er – dear me, you startled me!" said the man, in a very deep voice, with a decidedly foreign accent. "Yes, my boy, I own it. But, alas, it was a bad bargain. So few visitors come to see it."

"I suppose they come because they hope to hear the Wailing Banshee," said Fatty. "We heard it yesterday – a very fine performance, sir. Very fine. Best wailing I ever heard! How is it done, sir?"

"Done? My boy, who knows anything about the poor, poor unhappy banshees?" said the man. "Who knows how or why they wail?"

"Well, in these days, sir, I expect they wail because their machinery is started up," said Fatty, unexpectedly. "I mean – modern banshees are all pretence, aren't they?"

"Certainly NOT," said the man angrily. "You think I am a fraud? You think my banshee does not exist? I own a very fine banshee – poor poor thing, how she wails! It rends the heart!"

"Let me see now – banshees are supposed only to wail because they want to warn the owner of the place that something terrible is going to happen to him, aren't they?" said Fatty, putting on his most innocent

72

expression. "You know, sir, I heard her wailing yesterday, and I hoped somebody would warn you that trouble and unhappiness might be coming to you. Of course, that wouldn't be so if it wasn't a *real* banshee – but simply some kind of machinery, sir – but you are certain it isn't?"

"My boy, I give you leave to go into every room in Banshee Towers, and to look into every hole and corner and cranny there, to see if there is any machinery," said Mr. Engler, solemnly.

"Oh, thank you, sir, that's very kind of you, but I'll take your word for it that you've no machinery hidden in any of the rooms," said Fatty. "Let's change the subject, sir. What wonderful sea-pictures there are here! What collecion are they from, sir? I don't recognize any of them."

"Well, you seem to be an intelligent boy," said the Austrian, obviously struck by Fatty's ready conversation. "So I'll tell you. They are from a famous collection of pictures in Count Ludwig's castle in Austria. He is a cousin of mine, and he has lent me the pictures to attract visitors to Banshee Towers. A truly wonderful collection – but alas, few people look at the pictures. Just a few artists to copy them – and one or two visitors like yourself notice them."

"They are worth a lot of money, I suppose?" said Fatty.

"Oh yes, yes – thousands of pounds!" said Mr. Engler.

"I wonder you dare to risk the chance of some thief coming here to steal them," said Fatty.

"Now, my boy – use your sense," said Mr. Engler. "It is not easy to take great pictures like these from their frames and carry them off unnoticed! Ha – would *you* be able to do it?"

It was at this very moment that Ern decided to go

and find Fatty. Mr. Engler jumped when Ern's voice came into the room, sounding urgent.

"Fatty! Fatty, here! I've got something to ask you!"

"Excuse me, sir – that's my friend. I'd better go and see what he wants," said Fatty, surprised to see Ern looking so agitated. "Thank you for giving me so much information. Very kind of you."

He went over to Ern. "Ern! What is it? Now don't blurt it out at the top of your voice, for goodness sake. Come into the hall and tell me quietly."

"Well, Fatty, you know that sea-picture I liked so much – the one I showed you yesterday, with the high cliffs and the swirling sea below?"

"Yes, I remember it quite well. It's still over there," said Fatty, waving an arm towards it.

"Yes – well, there's something very queer about it today," said Ern, agitated. "Come and look."

"What do you mean – queer?" asked Fatty, surprised, as they came up to the picture.

"Something's gone out of it," said Ern. "Something I noticed particularly yesterday, Fatty. It's not there today, straight it isn't!"

"Well, what *was* it?" asked Fatty, exasperated. "The picture looks *exactly* the same to me!"

"Fatty, I promise you I'm telling the truth," said Ern. "I promise you! Now look – see that rock there – and the sea swirling up to it – and that wave coming up behind? Well, Fatty, *yesterday there was a little red boat painted* on that wave, with two tiny sailors in it. I noticed it particularly, and I thought to meself, well, the artist put in that boat just so's people looking at his picture would realize how enormous the cliffs were, and how grand the sea was, swirling round the rocks. See? If the artist hadn't put a boat there, I wouldn't have known how steep and high the cliffs were, so – so ..."

"So the picture would have lost some of its grandeur, you mean," said Fatty, with much interest. "Ern, this is, as you say, very queer. In fact, most peculiar. *Why* did someone paint out that boat? It must have been the Frenchman who did it, of course."

"Perhaps he doesn't like boats," said Ern. "Maybe he gets seasick. But Fatty, you can't see any marks where he might have washed the boat off the picture, or painted it out with greens or blues! That's what beats me!"

"It certainly is very strange," said Fatty, extremely puzzled. "You really *are* quite sure, Ern, that the boat was there yesterday?"

"Well, Bets was with me when we looked carefully at the picture." said Ern. "She liked the painting too. I expect she'd remember the boat all right. We'll ask her."

"Ern, listen – don't mention this to anyone – not to anyone at all." said Fatty. "I can't at the moment think why anyone should remove – or wash out – a boat from a sea-picture, but I'd like to think about it before we tell anyone. See?"

"Right," said Ern. "Now I'll go and look at some of the others. Maybe *all* the boats have been removed!" But no – those pictures that had boats in them, still had their boats – and their clouds – and their waves. Ern could see nothing missing in them. Nor could Fatty.

"Look – there's the Frenchman who was copying the picture yesterday," said Ern suddenly. "He's copying that small one over there now. Let's go and ask him if *he* removed that little boat from the big picture."

But before they could get to him, Mr. Engler, the Austrian, had gone over to him, and was in close conversation. Then the two men arose and went into the Armour Room, finally disappearing into a small room beyond.

"No banshee wailing today, Fatty," said Ern, with a grin, as they walked round the show of sea-pictures.

"Not the right day!" said Fatty, and immediately fell into such deep thought that he didn't hear a word of what Ern was saying to him. "*Not the right day?*" Why was one special day of the week the "right" day? Fatty didn't believe in the Banshee, even although he had felt very scared when it had wailed the day before.

"Ern, I have a feeling I'd like to go and have a look down that trap-door hole again," he said, suddenly. "You keep watch for me, see, and give a whistle if you see anyone coming. All the artists are gone except that Frenchman, and as far as I can see he's having a good heart-to-heart talk with Mr. Engler – goodness knows what about. I wish I did!"

He and Ern went into the Armour Room, and Ern stationed himself in the middle, so that he could watch all doors, and hear anyone approaching from any direction. Fatty went quietly to the great fireplace. He managed to move the cauldron to one side, and saw the trap-door underneath as before. He turned to Ern. "Everything safe?" he said, and Ern nodded. Not a footstep was to be heard anywhere, coming across the stone floors, not a voice echoed.

Fatty pulled up the trap-door lid, and peered down. Yes – there were steps leading downwards. To what? To the banshee – and maybe her machinery? Where was the *lower* entrance to this passage through the hill – the one the dogs must have found and taken to get up to Banshee Towers, and scrabble about under the trap-door? It must be a very well-hidden one, somewhere on the deserted hillside!

Fatty wished he dared to go down the steps and see what he could find. But he might be a long time gone, and he couldn't leave Ern behind. Nor did he want to take Ern with him. Neither of them had torches, and it would be dangerous.

He heard a sudden hiss from Ern, and stood up at once. There was just time to shut the trap-door and replace the great iron cauldron, so that the trap-door lid could not be seen!

Just in time! Footsteps sounded in the little room beyond, and voices. Mr. Engler and the artist were coming back! Fatty beckoned to Ern and the two fled into the hall and then through the turnstiles. The turnstile man was not there and to Fatty's surprise he suddenly saw him walking out of the hall-entrance with Mr. Engler and the artist!

"So they are all three buddies," thought Fatty. "Well, I don't know what it means, but it means *some*thing! I've got to work all this out, somehow. It's certainly adding up to a mystery of some sort – but I can't for the life of me see what or why or how!"

He and Ern went to get the two dogs, who, tired of being in the shed, were whining and pawing at the gate. They barked frantically and joyfully when the two boys came up. They hopped into their boxes on the rear mudguards and Fatty and Ern were soon sailing dangerously fast down the steep Banshee Hill.

"I think I'll call a Meeting tomorrow," Fatty said to Ern. "Something's going on up there that I can't make head or tail of. If we get the others to hear what we have to say and we all talk about it, we might see daylight. Good thing we went up, Ern, or you wouldn't have spotted the missing boat. I'm sure that's a clue to the mystery, whatever it is – but it's just about the most puzzling clue we've ever had! We don't even know what the mystery *is*, or if the clue really belongs to it. Whew!"

An interesting talk – and a good idea

Fatty telephoned Larry and Daisy that night, and also Pip and Bets. He would not tell them why the Meeting was being called, and they all felt rather excited. "Is it a Mystery, Fatty? Oh, do say it's another Mystery!" said Bets. "Have you any clues yet?"

"One," said Fatty. "And I don't even know what it's a clue *to* – or if it *is* a clue! Tell you all about it tomorrow. Be here at ten, please. Actually, it's a clue Ern found – I didn't even notice it!"

Just before ten o'clock there came knockings on the door of Fatty's workroom. He had lighted the stove, and had set out a variety of biscuits. As Fatty said, "It's so much *easier* to talk when you've got something to eat as well!"

In came Larry, Daisy, Pip and Bets, looking eager and excited. Buster and Bingo gave them a most uproarious greeting, and upset the plate of biscuits.

"Now listen, you two dogs," said Fatty, sternly, "I don't know which of you had the bright idea of upsetting biscuits all over the floor, but I tell you this – not *one* biscuit do you have till we've finished our Meeting. I know dogs consider it clever to upset plates of biscuits and cats think it is smart to upset milk, so that they can help themselves but I'm just a bit smarter than you are, see? SIT!"

The dogs sat eyeing the biscuits mournfully. Bets felt sorry for them and patted them. "Do begin the Meeting, Fatty," she said. "We're LONGING to hear about this new Mystery. Is it *really* one?"

"Well, that's what we're going to decide," said Fatty.

"If it is, we must make our plans to solve it. If it isn't, we just don't bother any more. Now, listen to what Ern discovered yesterday when we went up to Banshee Towers. Ern, would you like to take over – and tell what happened?"

"Oh, no thanks, Fatty," said Ern, uneasily. "You're the one to talk. There's nobody talks like you. I could listen for ages. My uncle, Mr. Goon always said you had the gift of the gab and he's right. You could talk the hind leg off a donkey, you could, or the tail off a horse, or the . . ."

"Well, really, Ern – anyone would think *you* had the gift of the gab," said Larry, surprised. "Do go on!"

"No," said Ern, and subsided. So Fatty took over, and began the tale of Ern's strange discovery.

"Ern went to look at that big sea-picture that he and Bets liked so much," he said. "Do you remember it, Bets?"

"Oh *yes* – every bit of it. It was lovely!" said Bets.

"Well describe it," said Fatty. "And don't leave even the smallest detail out, Bets. It's important."

"It was a picture of a stormy sea, with waves lashing against a very high cliff," said Bets. "The sky was blue in parts, and white in others. It was so full of spray that it almost made me feel wet."

"Anything else?" asked Fatty.

"Well no – except that there was a tiny red boat bobbing on a wave," said Bets. "When I saw that I suddenly realized how enormous the cliff was, and I thought the artist must have put it there on purpose – to make the cliff grander and the sea more – well, more magnificent, you know."

"Bets – that's just what we wanted you to remember – the *boat*," said Fatty, "because the boat is the only clue we have. That little boat is no longer in the picture. It's gone. It isn't there!"

79

There was an astonished silence. "Well, what's happened to it?" said Pip, at last. "Did some artist there wash it out – or paint over it? Perhaps he didn't like it?"

"No, he didn't wash it out, it seems," said Fatty. "There are *no* marks and *no* erasures. No – isn't that a peculiar little mystery?"

"It's impossible!" said Pip. "Perhaps Bets and Ern are mistaken – the little boat must have been in another of the sea-pictures. After all, there are masses of them up in that big hall."

"Yes. *That's* the solution!" said Larry. "It's obvious! Ern's mistaking one picture for another. There must be *another* picture there, with the little boat in it – there can't have been a boat in the one Ern thinks there was. Yes, I *know* that Bets saw it as well – but she too may have seen it in a different picture, that's all. After all, she didn't go up with you and Ern yesterday. If she had, she would probably have pointed out that it was in a different picture, and even taken you to it."

"I tell you," said Ern, exasperated, "I tell you the boat was in THAT PARTICULAR PICTURE I SAW YESTERDAY AND THE DAY BEFORE. I ought to know! I stood in front of it for ages. I feel as if I could almost paint the same picture myself!"

"All right, Ern, calm down," said Fatty. "Now, Find-Outers, any ideas?"

"You're *sure*, Ern, that it's the same picture, and is in exactly the same place?" asked Daisy. "Same cliffs, same waves, same sky, same frame, everything?"

"Same everything," said Ern, rather sulkily. "Goodness knows I looked at it long enough. It's just the *boat* that is missing – the little tiny boat."

"Well, I simply don't see any answer to this particular puzzle," said Fatty. "It's certainly a mystery – but rather a silly little mystery, with no rhyme or reason –

just a sea-picture from which a very small red boat has gone. We must give it up."

"The smallest mystery we've ever had, and the only one impossible to solve – what a pity!" said Larry.

"I think we *all* ought to pop up to Banshee Towers and have a look round to see if by any chance the picture with the boat has been hung somewhere else," said Daisy. "After all, some of the pictures look very alike – they are *all* sea-pictures with waves and cliffs and skies and ships. I'd rather like to solve this particular little mystery – not leave it in the air. It's a nice day – we could cycle up again."

"Yes. Let's do that," said Pip. "What do you say Ern?"

"Good idea," said Ern. "I'd like to find my little boat! Let's go now!"

And before long the six children were on their bicycles, once more on their way to Banshee Towers. A little Mystery like this was not going to beat the Find-Outers! They took the dogs too, in the boxes on Ern's and Fatty's back wheels. It was quite a little company, cycling along up the hill to Banshee Towers.

They were there at last – but what a shock! There was a notice up that said "CLOSED FOR TEMPORARY REPAIRS".

"Blow! Look at that!" said Ern, in dismay. "Now we shan't be able to find out about the boat."

It was indeed a blow. "Panting up that steep hill all for nothing!" groaned Pip. "Is the turnstile man anywhere about? He's a surly fellow, but he might let us in if we told him we only want to be there for half a minute."

"I wonder what repairs they are doing?" said Fatty. "The place seemed in very good order to me."

"Look – it's probably pipes they are replacing," said Larry, pointing to a pile of pipes of all sizes. "Looks as if their water-system has gone wrong. These are lead pipes – like we have in our houses at home. Probably the place is damp and you can't have damp in a picture-gallery. Ruins the pictures at once!"

"Yes. You're probably right," said Fatty, examining the pipes. "Well, Easter is over so they won't have many visitors till Whitsun – good time now to do any repairs. Well, what shall we do? Shall we just look round to see if *any*one's about?"

They wandered around, but saw no one. "What a waste of a morning," said Larry. "What can we do now?"

"I tell you what we *could* do, which would be rather fun," said Pip. "You remember how the dogs discovered some secret way up the hill, that led to the great fireplace in the Armour Room? They must have found an entrance somewhere on the hill – a cave or a hole of some sort – that had a passage leading to Banshee Towers! Can't we look for that?"

"Well, it *would* be fun," said Larry, and the others nodded. "Anyone brought a torch?"

Three of them had torches in their pockets. Good! "I don't expect there's much chance either of finding where the dogs made their way into the hill, or of getting up any passages ourselves," said Fatty. "It was probably nothing more than a large rabbit-hole they found, leading into some underground warren. Anyway – let's have a shot at finding it."

"The dogs will help," said Ern, and away they went on their bicycles down the hill with Bingo and Buster racing behind. Halfway down Fatty leapt off his bike, and called to Buster.

"Buster! Find! Find, Buster!"

Buster stood still with his ears pricked. *Find?* What was he to find? There were no rabbits here. He and

82

Bingo hadn't sniffed the scent of a single one. What *could* Fatty mean?

"Find, Buster! Find the hole you discovered the other day!" ordered Fatty. "FIND!"

He pointed here and there over the hill. Buster still stood with his ears cocked, his head on one side, trying his hardest to understand what his master wanted. It suddenly dawned on him that there was a hole somewhere – the hole he and Bingo had found – perhaps that was what Fatty wanted? A hole!

He gave a sharp little bark, and ran a little way uphill. He stood there, looking from side to side, sniffing the wind. Bingo came to join him, though he hadn't the faintest idea of what Fatty wanted.

Buster gave another short bark, and ran to the right, and then made for a great bush that overhung a steep part of the hill. Bingo followed, yapping.

"Come on – I think old Buster has understood what I meant," said Fatty, and he and the others climbed up the hill, soon becoming out of breath, for it was very steep just there. They had carefully hidden their bicycles under some thick bushes, a little lower down.

Both dogs had disappeared! Fatty yelled loudly. "BUSTER! Where are you? BUSTER!"

Buster appeared by the overhanging bush, and barked. Bingo appeared and barked too. What Buster did, he had to do as well!

"Come on," said Fatty. "I think Buster's found what we want! Whew – look here, under this bush – a great hole! I bet Buster thought it was a giant rabbit-hole. I have a feeling that this is where *we* disappear – into the heart of the hill. Let's hope we come up in the right place! Follow me, everybody!"

And there they go, one by one. Be careful, Fatty – there may be danger ahead!

Up the passage – and a queer find!

The hole was quite a large one, with long grass and some kind of creeping plant growing across the entrance. Fatty, bent double, pushed his way into it, shining his torch in front of him. He could hear Buster and Bingo scrabbling some way ahead, giving little woofs, as if chatting with each other.

The hole became much larger after a few yards, and Fatty was able to straighten himself a little and make his way more comfortably. He soon saw that the passage he was in was now of rock, not of earth. It was very uneven, and at times the roof came down so low that he had to bend almost double.

Behind him came Bets, then Larry, then Daisy, Ern and Pip being the last two. Larry and Pip held the other torches, which gave a very good light in the black darkness of the strange passage. Ahead were the two dogs, very pleased and excited to think that Fatty and the others were using the passage they had found some days before!

"My word – isn't it steep!" shouted Fatty, and made the others jump – for his voice sounded very strange in the narrow passage – not at all like Fatty's usual voice! It was muffled and mysterious, and had a queer echo.

"Steep-tee-eep!" came the echo. The dogs didn't like it. They stopped, pricked their ears, and whined.

"It's all right, Buster," said Fatty. "Only the echo. Carry on!"

"Carry-on, arry-on – on – on!" said the echo, and the dogs barked angrily. That was worse still, of course! The rocky passage was immediately full of wild barks,

84

and the dogs were very frightened indeed. Was this place full of hundreds of dogs? They made their way back to Fatty in alarm, and he patted them, and spoke quietly, trying to defeat the curious echo.

"Now, now – it's all right. Good dogs! VERY good dogs! Go on now – show us the way."

"Way," said the echo, also quietly. "Way-way-waaaaay!"

After they had all climbed a good while, very glad indeed of their torches, Fatty stopped for a rest. The last bit had been very steep indeed. He waited until the others had come up close, and then spoke.

"We *should* be near Banshee Towers now," he said. "You remember that there is a trap-door under the old cauldron – well, that means that any noise we make now may echo up into the Armour Room. So be very quiet, please – just in case anyone is there."

Without a word, and making as little noise as possible, the six went climbing up. Fatty made the dogs keep close to him, so that he could prevent them barking.

But before they came to the trap-door they came to something that surprised them very much! Fatty saw it first, of course, because he was leading. His torch suddenly showed him a big space just in front, and he stopped in surprise. The tunnel had widened out into a kind of underground room – a room with an uneven rocky floor, and equally uneven rocky walls. Fatty was able to stand completely upright. He shone his torch round the underground room in surprise.

He gave a short whistle. "Whew! What's all this? Quick, everyone, come and look!"

They crowded into the strange rocky room. It was quite empty except for three things: a piece of peculiar-looking machinery – something that looked like a deflated balloon – and a chair!

"What on *earth* is all this?" said Pip, shining his torch on the machinery.

"At a guess I should say it was the machinery that sets the dear old banshee wailing at the top of her voice!" said Fatty.

"Are you sure?" said Bets. "What's that balloon thing for? Shine your torch on it, Fatty."

"I should think that this balloon is inflated by a pump worked by that bit of machinery," said Fatty. "And then, when it *de*flates, it makes that screaming, wailing banshee noise."

"But how is it that it's heard all over Banshee Towers?" asked Bets, puzzled.

"Oh, there are probably amplifiers in every room," said Fatty, who always seemed to know everything. "You know – things that magnify any sound, and make it tremendously loud. Don't you remember how loud the wailing was when we heard it the other day? And how clear and distinct it was?"

"Oh yes," said Bets, shivering as she remembered the horrible noise. "But Fatty – what a peculiar thing to do – to fill the place with wails like that! I should have thought it would frighten people away – not bring them here!"

"Yes. It seems a bit odd when you put it like that, Bets," said Fatty, fiddling about with the machinery. "I wonder how this works. What's this wheel for?"

He turned the wheel to the right. Nothing happened. He turned it to the left – and, very suddenly indeed, something began to work inside the machinery – clank – click – clonk – click – clunk . . .

"It's working! Turn it off, quick!" cried Bets, afraid of what might happen. But Fatty didn't. He watched the machine, a little grin on his face. Oh, Fatty, Fatty – you know quite well what you've done!

The balloon-thing began to move. Buster saw it trembling, and he growled and showed his teeth. Bingo immediately did the same. The balloon grew bigger and bigger – and then came another loud click, and something fell into place and began whirring. The children couldn't see what it was.

"I bet that's the amplifier getting ready to work!" said Fatty, his eyes gleaming. "We'll hear something in a minute. Don't be scared, little Bets. It's only machinery Ah – here we go!"

And then, from the now fully-inflated balloon, came a weird, unhappy sound – a wailing that held everyone spellbound, it seemed so human! Bets took Fatty's hand at once, frightened at the strange noise. It sounded so very very heart-rending.

"It's only a very clever trick, Bets," said Fatty, in a low voice. "Just a bit of machinery – and a specially fitted-up balloon – and an amplifier to make the wails very loud indeed. All fitted neatly into a most convenient underground hole in a rock. I wonder if Mr. Engler is at the bottom of this!"

"Oh, Fatty – PLEASE stop the machine!" begged Bets. "I HATE this wailing. I HATE it."

Fatty pulled a little lever. The machinery slowed down. The balloon gradually deflated. The wailing grew slower and softer, and then stopped altogether. There was a marvellous silence, and everyone enjoyed the sudden peace. Bets heaved an enormous sigh.

"Ooooooooo! I shall never hear a more horrible noise in all my life thán that wailing. Fatty, no real banshee could ever have wailed like that, surely."

"I should find it very difficult to believe in a real banshee, Bets," said Fatty, examining the machinery carefully, by the light of his torch. "I even find it difficult to believe in a man like Engler, who is wicked enough to rig up a thing like this. But unfortunately, *he's* real enough! Well, what do we do now?"

"Fatty, please let's go up through the trap-door if we can, and have a look at those pictures again," begged Ern. "I do want to see if Bets remembers the one that the boat was in. If she does, I'll know I'm right about it. If she doesn't – well, then there's no mystery. I'm beginning to hope there isn't! What with banshees, and disappearing boats, and hidden machinery I feel rather sick!"

"Well, don't be sick in here Ern, there really isn't room!" said Fatty, briskly. "Right – we'll go up through the trap-door – providing nobody's about. But I think that if there had been, we should have had a visitor down here pretty quickly, trying to find out WHY the banshee wailed all on her own! I have a feeling that the place really *is* shut up today."

Fatty went to an opening in the furthest wall of the queer little rock-room, and shone his torch into it. "Just as I thought!" he announced. "Steps! Steps cut into the rock, just like a ladder! I bet it's the steps we saw leading down from that hole in the hearth, where the trap-door was!"

The others crowded round him. Yes – there were the steps that they had seen the other day from above! "I'll go first," said Fatty. "Better make no noise, just in *case* anyone's about. But I feel certain there isn't, or whoever was here would have come rushing to see why the banshee machinery was suddenly working!"

Everyone was silent as Fatty climbed the rocky steps. He soon came to the top, but could see nothing above his head but the trap-door set firmly in its place. "Here goes!" said Fatty, and gave it a push upwards. It upset the iron cauldron standing over it and this fell over on its side with a terrific clatter that scared Fatty almost as much as it frightened the others down below!

He stood at the top of the steps, listening. To his enormous relief he could hear nothing – no shouts of surprise, no clatter of running feet – nothing! The place must be completely empty. Well, thank goodness for *that*!

Fatty climbed out of the trap-door hole and looked round. The place seemed absolutely deserted. Well, now they could examine the pictures to their heart's content – and maybe solve the mystery of the missing boat!

One by one he hauled the others up from the hole in the hearth. The dogs were handed up last of all by Ern, and were very glad to scurry around and stretch their legs properly! How they had hated that wailing!

"I want to look at that lovely sea-picture," said Bets, at once. "Ern, come with me."

She and Ern hurried through the Armour Room into the great hall where the pictures hung. Yes – there they all were, in their blues and greens, sunshiny, stormy, windy, some of them stretching from floor to ceiling.

"Here's that boat-picture," called Ern, standing in front of it. "Do you remember it, Bets?"

"Oh *yes*!" said Bets. "Yes – there was a little red boat that's not there now. I *know* there was one, Ern, it was on this wave here, wasn't it?" And Bets touched one of the waves not far from the bottom of the picture.

"Yes!" said Ern, triumphantly. "That's *exactly* where it was, Bets. I told you that, didn't I, Fatty? Now Bets has told you too. We can't both be wrong!"

"Fatty – where do you think the boat has gone?" said Bets, really puzzled. "It doesn't look as if it's been washed out or painted over."

"A big wave probably caught it and it sank to the bottom," said Pip, solemnly. "That's the simplest explanation, Bets."

"Don't be so *silly*!" said Bets, quite worried over the vanished boat. "Fatty, I'd like to look at some of the other pictures too."

But before they could do that, dogs, who had

been wandering happily about together, suddenly stood still and began to growl, their hackles rising on their necks. Fatty shushed everyone at once.

"Get back into the Armour Room, girls. Somebody's coming!" he whispered. "Buck up. You'll have to get down the trap-door quickly, and run for your lives! We shall be in real trouble if we're found here. Larry and Pip, look after the girls!"

The two girls shot off into the Armour Room with Pip and Larry, and were soon down the steps. They wanted to wait for Ern and Fatty, but Larry wouldn't let them. "You're in my charge now," he said. "Quickly now – get along underground!"

Fatty too went to the Armour Room with Ern, hoping there would be time for them both to slip down the hole. But there wasn't! He just managed to push the cauldron quickly over the trap-door and step back on to the hearth-rug.

Footsteps came to the door of the room and a voice snapped out. "Stand where you are! What's all this? How did you get in, you boys! Answer me at once!"

Prisoners – now what can be done?

It was Mr. Engler who stood there, shouting! He looked extremely angry, and his face was very red. Behind him stood the turnstile man, a sneering smile on his face. Buster flew at them, with Bingo behind him, and both dogs were kicked hard by the two men, and howled in pain.

"Call off these dogs, or I'll kill them," said Mr. Engler, pulling a great sword from the wall, where it had been hanging.

"SIT, Buster, SIT, Bingo!" shouted Fatty, his heart cold with fear. To his enormous relief both dogs sat at once, growling savagely, their hackles still up. Thank goodness Buster had been trained to be instantly obedient, thought Fatty. Bingo, of course, had just copied Buster. How fierce they both looked, showing their teeth, longing to get at these two men who dared to shout at Fatty and Ern.

"Good thing they obey you," said Mr. Engler, still holding the sword. "I like dogs, or I wouldn't give them a chance. Now explain your presence here, please. The door was locked – so I presume you came in through one of the windows. I saw that one was open when I came – the one on the first floor. Easy enough to climb up ivy, isn't it – easy to break into a place. You boys will have to explain all that when you come before the police!"

Fatty was thankful that the man thought they had broken in through an open window. He said nothing. He was certainly not going to explain about the trap-door in the hearth! If the man didn't know of it, well and good!

"Oh, don't take us to the police, sir," blurted out Ern, thinking of Goon's face, if he, Ern, were taken to the police station. "Please don't. We weren't doing any harm, reely we weren't. We were just looking round, like."

"I've seen these kids before, sir," said the turnstile man. "Cheeky lot they are, too. Six of them have been coming up – with these dogs. I *told* them dogs weren't allowed. I was a bit afraid these kids might find out what we . . ."

"Shut up, Flint, you fool!" snapped Mr. Engler, clearly afraid that he was about to say something he didn't want the boys to hear. "Go and begin to load the van, and be sharp about it. I'll deal with what's not ready, and you can fetch it later."

He turned to the two listening boys. "I'm afraid you are going to have a very poor week-end," he said. "I've decided *not* to hand you over to the police – but to leave you all alone here, without food or drink for two or three days. Just to teach you what happens to lads who break into places! Oh, you needn't think you can get out of the window you so easily slipped in by! I shall tie you up and lock you in this room, and when I come back on Monday – or maybe Tuesday – I'll listen to your apologies and let you go – perhaps!"

"But, sir – our parents will be so worried," began Fatty. "We haven't done any harm. We apologize *now*. We do really. Don't we, Ern?"

"Ooooh yes," said Ern, fervently, a little surprised to hear Fatty talking in such a humble voice. Why, Fatty sounded *scared*! "First time I've ever seen him frightened," thought Ern.

"You can apologize when you next see me, and have had time to think what fools you have both been," said Mr. Engler. The turnstile man grinned sarcastically. He was very, very glad to see that "cheeky fat boy" as he thought of him, standing there, caught so easily.

"Tie them up," said Mr. Engler, to the turnstile man. "I'm going to see if Poussin is there. He's about due now."

Fatty wondered who Poussin was. It was a French name, so maybe it was the French artist. He stood waiting for the turnstile man to tie up him and Ern. "Got to go and get some rope, if you want me to tie them up," said the man, turning.

"No. Use those curtain cords," said Mr. Englar. "I must go and see if Poussin has come. These boys are not to be left alone until their wrists are tied tightly, behind their backs! TIGHTLY, I said, Flint. And DON'T talk to them – else I'll talk to *you*! Do you hear me?"

"Yes," said Flint, sulkily, and went to tear down the

cords that pulled the great curtains open or shut. He had soon tied the boys by their wrists and ankles very tightly indeed.

"You know these cords are too tight," said Fatty, between his teeth. "No need to be so brutal."

"Ha – you're not so funny now, are you!" said Flint. "Cheeking me out there, you was. Don't feel like cheeking me now, do you?"

Fatty heard another voice – the French artist's. He was in the great hall, with Engler. He was speaking in French, which Fatty understood perfectly. He strained his ears to listen. He was extremely surprised to hear noises as of a ladder being dragged along the hall, and set up somewhere. He listened hard. *That* sounded like a knife being used to cut something. What on earth were they doing? Not damaging the pictures, surely!

Then he thought he heard the sound of a brush being slapped over some surface. A brush? A *paint*-brush probably. Was the Frenchman painting a picture out there, his easel set up as usual? No, it couldn't be that – he wouldn't *slap* the paint on!

Flint, the turnstile man, finished tying Ern's wrists, stood back and grinned at the two angry boys. "Well – happy dreams!" he said. "And may the rats and mice run all over you tonight! This place is full of them."

"You wait till we see you again," said Fatty. "We'll be handing you over to the police, I hope! What are you all up to? Beats me!"

"You won't see *me* again – I'm off to the States!" said Flint. "America's the place for me now. We'll soon be off – and the old banshee can wail her head off for us, we shan't hear her!"

He went out, banged the door, and the boys heard the key being turned in the lock. Ern groaned as he lay trussed up on the floor beside Fatty.

"This is a nice how-do-you-do," he said. "Good thing the men don't guess we . . ."

"Shut up, Ern," hissed Fatty. "They may be listening, hoping we'll give something away. Can you stand up?"

"No," said Ern, trying. "Hallo, Bingo – pity you can't untie me. Is Buster clever enough to untie *you*, Fatty? Have you taught him things like that yet?"

Buster and Bingo were puzzled and distressed to see Fatty and Ern rolling on the floor, groaning as their cords seemed to get tighter and tighter. They licked the boys' faces, and whined pitifully. Fatty rolled to a settee and by means of using his tied hands, managed to get himself into a sitting position. He then stood up on his tied feet and began to hop to a window that overlooked the yard outside.

He was interested to see a small van there – a plain dark blue one. Flint, the turnstile man, must have just finished loading it, for he was at that moment slamming the door at the back. Then he went to the front, hopped into the driver's seat, and started up the engine. At the same time a car drove up behind it, and the two drove off together. Fatty quickly memorized the numbers of the van and of the car.

"JBL 333 – and POR 202," he muttered. "Gosh, I wish I could write those numbers down – I'll never remember them. Ern, can you remember JBL 333 and POR 202?"

"I don't think so," said poor Ern. "I can't think of anything but my wrists and ankles. Fatty, what are we going to do? We'll never be able to get these cords off."

"Of course we shall!" said Fatty. "I didn't want to get them off before those fellows went – I was afraid they might come back at any moment."

94

Fatty spent ages trying to undo Ern's cords.

"But HOW can we get our hands free?" said Ern. "The cord's much too strong!"

Fatty hopped across to the wall, where a curious foreign knife hung. He raised his wrists behind his back and placed them so that the cords were against the edge of the knife. Very gently he began to rub the cords up and down the knife, careful not to press too hard and cut himself.

Ern watched him in admiration. Trust old Fatty to think of something smart! Fatty worked away and finally felt one cord give – then another. He pulled hard, and very thankfully felt the cords loosening and slipping off his hands.

"My word, my hands are all numb and stiff," he said, trying to bend them this way and that. "I'll undo yours, Ern, when I can feel some life in my fingers."

Buster ran to him and licked Fatty's hands, whining. He knew Fatty was in some kind of trouble and his doggy mind was upset and worried. There didn't seem to be anything at all that he could do for Fatty.

It was some time before Fatty could use his hands, and even then they were shockingly painful. He spent ages trying to undo Ern's cords. He dared not use the knife on them, for his hands were now too numb to use a knife safely.

But at last Ern's cords were undone too. His hands were worse than Fatty's, for Flint had tied them very viciously. Soon their ankles were untied as well, and life began to seem a little brighter.

"Are we going to escape down the underground passage?" asked Ern. "I don't think I can walk, though. My legs are all pins and needles and I can't feel my feet."

"The girls and Pip and Larry will send help for us," said Fatty. "What *I'd* like to do is to get out of this room and wander round some of the upstairs rooms.

I have a feeling we might find something interesting there!"

"That fellow locked the door. I heard him," said Ern.

"I know – but we *might* be able to get to it, and unlock it from *this* side," said Fatty. He walked unsteadily to the door and looked at the lock. Then he bent down and looked *under* the door. Ern watched him in interest. What was old Fatty up to now?

"I'm going to use an old trick – one I've used before, Ern," said Fatty. He went to the table and took a catalogue from the pile there. He tore out the middle pages, leaving only the stiff outer covers. These he took over to the door, knelt down again and pushed them flat underneath it, so that the greater part of the covers was on the other side of the door.

Then he stood up, and, with the end of his penknife blade, juggled the key in the lock until it was in a position for him to give it a push, and send it out on the other side of the door! The key promptly fell out – and there was a little thud as it landed on the floor at the bottom of the door. Buster and Bingo barked loudly. What was happening now?

"Good!" said Fatty, pulling at the piece of stiff cover showing under the door on his side. Carefully he pulled it towards him, oh so gently – and, as the stiff covers came under the door, *the key lying on them came too!* There it was at last, safely on their side of the door. "Now," said Fatty, "We can unlock the door from *our* side, and do a little exploring! Come on, Ern. Can you walk all right?"

Fatty picked up the key that he had so carefully pulled under the bottom of the door. "Hope I can turn it!" he said, making a face as he put the key in the lock. "My wrist feels as if it hasn't even the strength to turn a key if the lock is stiff!"

But the key turned easily! Fatty opened the door and peered out cautiously into the Picture Hall. He knew that he had seen the car and the van go off but he didn't want to run into anyone who might still be in the place.

All was quiet. Buster and Bingo, very much on guard, stood close by the boys, ready to growl and fly at anyone who might be going to hurt them.

"There can't be anybody here now," said Fatty. "The dogs would be growling if there were. Hallo – look, there's a step-ladder over there – and a tin of something, with a brush in it. Looks as if somebody's been up to something. You remember we heard a ladder being pulled across the floor, Ern – and the slapping of a brush?"

They were puzzled when they came to the tin. They had expected it to be full of paint – but it wasn't! "It's some kind of gluey-paste," said Fatty, dipping his finger into the tin. "My word – don't get it on your clothes, Ern – it's about the strongest paste or glue I've ever felt. I just can't get it off my finger! Now – what on earth was it used for?"

They gazed at the two sea-pictures on each side of the tin. Nothing to help them there – but wait a minute! Fatty suddenly noticed a thin, shining streak of what looked like something sticky down the inner side of one of the frames. He touched it. It *was* sticky!

He was very puzzled. Why had someone used glue of some kind – had the frame cracked, and needed a little glueing? Pictures weren't *glued* into their frames – they were backed with board, and then the frames were neatly placed over them. Fatty gave up, putting the strange fact into a corner of his mind to consider later.

"Come on, Fatty – what are you dreaming about, standing there gazing down at that tin of glue, or whatever it is," said Ern, impatiently. "I want to get out of this place. So do the dogs!"

Bingo was whining. He didn't like Banshee Towers. He wanted to have a good long run and stretch his legs.

"All right, Bingo, old thing," said Fatty. "We'll soon be off and away. I just want to have a little look round – a 'snoop' is a better name, perhaps – and see if I can unearth a few of Mr. Engler's queer little secrets!"

They went to a big staircase that had a very large board at the bottom with the words "PRIVATE. NO ENTRY."

Fatty took not the slightest notice of the big board, but went straight up the stairs. He went rather slowly, and so did Ern, for their ankles were still swollen and painful after the cruelly tight cords. The dogs raced up before them, barking.

They came to a big room. There was a large desk there, and a smaller one. Pictures and empty frames were stacked all over the place. There was a great pile of catalogues on the big desk, and scattering of letters.

"Very interesting," said Fatty, turning over the canvases on which various pictures had been painted. "All sea-pictures, of course. Look here, Ern – remember this one?"

"Yes, it's a double of the one we saw in the frame by the tin of glue," he said. "Can't see any difference!

99

That's a copy, I suppose. Done by that French artist. That's all he did, seems to me – sit there and copy somebody else's pictures! Funny – I should have thought a *real* artist wouldn't want to copy."

"He might – if he were well paid, Ern," said Fatty. "Hallo – here's a pile of letters all neatly stacked together and tied with pink tape. Let's have a look and see who they're from!"

"Do you think you ought to look at other people's letters?" said Ern, uncomfortably.

"Oh, I think that after the kind of treatment the spiteful Mr. Engler served out to us he really can't complain of anything *we* do!" said Fatty, reading some of the letters. "In any case, Ern, I intend to give them to Inspector Jenks. He will be very pleased indeed to have them."

"Coo!" said Ern, astonished. "I wouldn't say that, Fatty. He might lock you up for taking them. Better leave them here."

Fatty took no notice. He was absorbed in one or two of the letters. Ern peeped at the heading on each. "The Hedling Art Gallery, Diddinghame, U.S.A." was one. "Art Shows Company, New York, U.S.A." was another. "Grand Pictures Company, Hinkling, U.S.A." a third. "Gracious!" though Ern. "What does Fatty think he can find in letters like that!"

He peeped down a sheet that Fatty was absorbed in reading, but couldn't make head or tail if it. "Just a list of pictures, and prices and artists," thought Ern. He spoke aloud.

"Fatty, I reckon we're just wasting time now. Let's go. Those fellows might come back sooner then we expect – and anyway Bets and the others might already be sending help to us, you know. That'd be a waste of time, seeing that we can just walk out and go home when we want to!"

100

"Right Ern," said Fatty. "Just let me make a list of the Art Galleries listed here that buy pictures from Engler." He scribbled quickly, and then took a last look round. "We'll just peep in the room next door first. I have a feeling we still haven't seen quite all I expected to see."

They went into the next room, a smaller one. Ern stared in surprise. It was fitted up as a very comfortable bedroom! A large wardrobe stood open, showing many clothes hanging there. Thrown across an unmade bed was a dark painting overall, covered with smudges of oil-paint. A book lay on a table beside the bed.

Fatty picked it up. "At a guess I should say this book was a French one!" he said. He looked down at it and nodded. "Yes – all about famous Continental pictures – especially pictures of the sea!" Fatty turned to the flyleaf at the beginning of the book. "And here the owner has kindly written his name – it belongs to that French Artist, of course – and here is his address – François Henri Ortalo, 91, Rue Carnot, Paris. Very nice of him to leave it so handy! Interesting to see that Mr. Engler has given him such a nice room to live in, too. He must be very useful to him!"

"Oh, do stop messing about with books and letters!" said Ern desparingly. "I want to go! I hate this place. At any moment I expect to hear that awful banshee-wail."

"All right, Ern, we'll go," said Fatty, scribbling quickly again in his notebook. "I think we'd better make ourselves scarce, anyway, in case Mr. Engler pops back again through the front door. I don't feel inclined to meet him again today. I don't like his manners!"

"He's a beast," said Ern "My ankles still feel as if I've been running for miles, they ache so, where they were tied."

"Ah well," said Fatty, snapping shut his notebook.

"We'll soon forget our wrists and ankles. Actually I'm feeling rather bucked, I think I've now got the whole mystery wrapped up very neatly indeed!"

"You're boasting Fatty!" said Ern, disbelievingly. "What about the little painted boat that disappeared from that picture downstairs? I bet you don't know how *that* happened?"

"Well, we'll see," said Fatty. "I really think I'm beginning to see daylight! We'll go home now and find the others and tell them what we've found. Let's see – they had to escape down that underground passage in the hill – and find their bikes – and then ride home."

"Well, unless they stopped on the way to have ice-creams or something, they will be home before us," said Ern.

"They'd hardly stop for ice-creams when they knew we were in trouble!" said Fatty.

"No, I forgot that," said Ern. "Come on – let's go downstairs, slip out of the front door with the dogs, and run down the hill to where we left our bikes underneath that bush."

They went down the stairs with the two excited dogs, both wagging their tails madly, though as Ern pointed out, Bingo's tail *waved* rather than wagged, it was so very very long.

They opened the front door and slipped out, shutting it quietly behind them. They made their way cautiously down the hill, keeping close to the hedges, half-afraid of seeing Mr. Engler and his companions somewhere about. The two dogs, sensing that all was not quite right with their masters, pressed close to their heels, and didn't even attempt to go sniffing for rabbits.

At last they came to where they had left their bicycles, hidden in bushes. They looked round for the bicycles belonging to the other four, but they were gone.

"Good – then they got down the banshee passage safely," said Fatty. "They can't really be very much in front of us now – we were pretty quick down that hill!"

They were soon riding fast down the rest of the hill, the dogs bumping in their boxes behind. It was a miracle that they didn't fall out, for the boys went so fast.

"What do we do when we get back?" shouted Ern. "I hope you won't go and report everything to my Uncle Goon. I wouldn't like that. You know I'm in trouble with him!"

"Don't worry, Ern. We hold all the winning cards now," shouted back Fatty, comfortably. "I rather think we ought to go over Goon's head, and get in touch with Chief Inspector Jenks. We know him quite well enough. This is a bit too big a thing for a village policeman to handle."

"Luvaduck!" said Ern, in awe. "But won't the Chief Inspector think it's a bit cheeky of us to telephone him? I mean, he's a Big Noise, he is."

"We'll get back to my shed first," said Fatty, freewheeling very fast. "And find out where the others are. They can't have been back very long. My word, Ern – I'm beginning to feel bucked. I'm seeing daylight! The Mystery is dissolving – everything FITS!"

"Go on, Fatty!" said Ern, disbelievingly. "It's just a muddle to me, straight it is! The only fits *I* know are the ones I'll have when my uncle gets hold of me! Oooh, Fatty, go slower – old Bingo nearly shot out of his box just then. FATTY!"

Fatty and Ern arrived at Fatty's home safely, much to Buster's relief. Part of the road had been so bumpy that poor Buster had found himself wishing he had sharp cat-claws to hold on with, instead of his own blunt ones! He had decided that he didn't want to go bicycling with Fatty ever again. Bicycling and dogs didn't really go very well together!

He and Bingo jumped gladly out of the boxes tied on to the back mudguards, and Buster went to see if anyone had put something good into his enamel bowl. Ah – kind old Cookie! She had filled his bowl with some nice fresh meat. Bingo rushed up too – and, hungry as he was, Buster remembered his manners, and allowed Bingo to share.

"Good, Buster, I'm pleased with you," said Fatty. "We'll buy a good dollop of meat for Bingo, and I'm sure he'll share his with you too. Now you two dogs stay out here."

He opened the door of his shed. No one was there! "Where are the others?" he said, looking round. "Gosh – I hope they're all right. What's happened to them? We certainly didn't pass them on the way!"

"Perhaps one of them had a puncture," said Ern – and as it happened, he was quite right! Larry's front tyre suddenly went flat, and he and the others had stopped at a little opening in a nearby wood, while Larry mended the puncture.

Ern and Fatty had actually cycled past them, and hadn't even seen them, or heard their shouts!

"You simply *whizzed* by," complained Larry, when

at last he and the others arrived at Fatty's workroom. "We yelled and shouted, but you were gone – psssst! like that! Sixty miles an hour – and the two dogs bumping up and down like apples in a basket!"

"Fatty, are you all right? What happened when we left you?" said Bets. "I was so afraid those men might hurt you!"

"Oh, *we* were all right," said Fatty, hurriedly pulling his coat sleeves down as far as they would go, to hide the painful red lines round his wrists. "We found out a whole lot of interesting things, Bets. We must have a Meeting at once!"

But before they could really settle down to it, someone came knocking at the shed door, opened it and looked in. "Frederick, are you there? There's someone on the telephone for you."

"Oh, Mother, can't you say I'm busy or something!" said Fatty, exasperated. "We're JUST starting a most *important* Meeting. *Really* important."

"All right dear, I'll go back and tell Chief Inspector Jenks what you say," said his mother, and shut the door.

But Fatty leapt up with a yell. "MOTHER! Wait! You didn't say it was Inspector Jenks! Mother, I'm coming straightaway!"

Ern looked round at the others, as Fatty shot out of the door at top speed, Buster at his heels. "I bet the Inspector's heard of our discoveries at Banshee Towers," he said, pleased. "I expect he wants to ask Fatty a whole lot of questions. Funny how old Fatty always seems to get in on things first, isn't it? My word, you wait till Fatty tells you what we discovered this morning!"

Fatty ran all the way up the garden to his house, his mind going over likely reasons for the Chief Inspector's telephone call.

"Probably he's heard about the Banshee Towers'

goings-on – the wailing banshee, for instance – and maybe he's suspicious of Mr. Engler's doing. Well, I can certainly give him some up-to-date information," thought Fatty, feeling pleased.

He ran to the telephone and picked up the receiver. "Chief Inspector Jenks? Frederick Trotteville here, sir. Sorry to keep you waiting."

"Frederick, I'll come to the point at once," said the Chief. "I'm sorry to say I've had a serious complaint about you. I expect you have a perfectly good explanation, and I sincerely hope you have."

Fatty felt most alarmed. "What's all this about, sir?" he asked, bewildered.

"Well, actually there are *two* complaints!" said the Chief. "One, *not* very serious, from Mr. Goon, about Ern, who, he says, was put in his charge by Ern's mother and who has run away and is being harboured by you in your shed."

"That's quite right, sir," said Fatty, at once. "And I'm sure you won't blame me, sir. Goon went for poor old Ern, and he . . ."

"I'm afraid Ern will have to go *back* to Goon," said the Chief. "It's his mother's wish – and parents do have *some* rights, you know."

"All right, sir. I'll see to it," said Fatty, feeling very, very sorry for Ern.

"The second complaint, Frederick," said the clear voice down the telephone, "the second complaint is much more serious. It's been put in by a Mr. Engler, the owner of Banshee Towers. He accuses you of breaking into the Towers, with another boy, whose name he doesn't know – and there are also two dogs complained of. Apparently dogs are not allowed inside, and you were told this – and yet you were found there with a *couple*! Whose is the second dog?"

"Ern's," said Fatty, in a small voice. His heart was

106

sinking down and down and down.

"ERN'S! I didn't even know he *had* a dog!" said the Chief.

"Yes, sir, he has. Called Bingo," said Fatty.

"What on *earth* were you and Ern and two dogs doing wandering about Banshee Towers?" demanded the Chief. "Apparently it was closed for the day, and the doors were locked. Frederick, surely you *didn't* break in anywhere?"

"Well, not exactly *break* in, if you mean smash locks or windows or anything like that," said poor Fatty. "We certainly did *get* in – we . . ."

The Chief gave a deep groan. "You are a very, very foolish boy, Frederick. You have played right into this fellow Engler's hands. He is a smart, spiteful, clever crook. We've been trying to pin something on him – and now you've messed things up by putting yourself in *his* hands, Frederick. I simply do not know how I'm going to get you out of this fix."

"I know he's a crook, sir," said Fatty, in a small voice. "We were trying to catch him out sir – that phoney banshee wailing, for instance, and . . ."

"*You* knew he was a crook!" said the Chief, very surprised. "How on earth . . . look here, Frederick, I'd better come round and see you. I simply never know what you are up to. The sooner you grow up and join the police force so that I can *really* keep my eye on you, the better. Stay at home till I come. That's an order, see?"

He slammed down the telephone, and Fatty put back his own receiver, most surprised to find his hand shaking. Gosh – this wasn't funny at all. What in the world would his father say?

"I suppose I must be getting a bit too big for my boots," said Fatty to himself. "My word, I've never heard the Chief go off the handle like that before! Did

I feel a worm? Yes, I certainly did. I only wish I had a nice, deep hole to go to!"

He called to his mother. "Mother! The Inspector will be along in a little while. Will you tell him we're down in my shed, please?"

Then away he went, hoping that his mother wouldn't call him back and ask him awkward questions. He opened the door of his shed, and went in.

"You look gloomy, Fatty. What's up?" said Bets, at once. Fatty sank down dramatically into a chair, sighed and passed his hand over his forehead.

"Well, I rather think I may have to go to prison – or to Borstal or somewhere," he said. "Old man Engler has put in a complaint about me – charged me with Breaking and Entering Banshee Towers. And Mr. Goon has *also* put in a complaint – that when Ern ran away, I 'harboured' him."

"You never harboured me!" said Ern, who hadn't the faintest idea of what "harbouring" really meant. "I'm not a ship! You just gave me board and lodging, Fatty – let me stay here in your shed."

"Well – that's another way of saying that I 'harboured' you – gave you shelter," said Fatty.

Ern jumped up at once. "I'll go back to my uncle's then," he said. "I won't let you get punished because you've been kind to *me*, Fatty! That's not fair!"

"Sit down, Ern," said Fatty. "We can't do anything for the moment. Chief Inspector Jenks is coming along here soon. I'll have to wait for him. I'd like you all to stay, though."

"Is my uncle coming too?" said Ern, fearfully.

"I don't think so," said Fatty. "Gosh – wouldn't *I* like to put in a complaint about your *uncle*, Ern. In fact I can think of several complaints I could put in."

"Nothing to what *I* could think of," said Ern, gloomily. "Shouting at me and almost deafening me. Clipping

108

me on the ear. Pushing me around. Taking my . . ."

"Listen – someone's coming," said Fatty, his ears even sharper then than those of the dogs. "I heard a car draw up outside our front gate. I'm sure."

"You couldn't have, Fatty!" said Larry. "It's right down the garden, and . . ."

But just then the two dogs set up such a loud barking that nobody could hear anyone speak. "SHUT UP!" shouted Fatty, making a dive for Buster. "Do you want me to be had up for creating a noisy disturbance, Buster! Ern, get hold of Bingo. They both seem to have gone mad."

A loud knock came at the shed door, and the two dogs almost barked the place down. Then the door opened and there stood Chief Inspector Jenks, tall, burly, keen-eyed – but not smiling as he usually was. He looked round the little company.

"Oh – so *all* the Find-Outers are here, are they?" he said, and smiled. Fatty was most relieved to see that smile. Perhaps the Inspector wasn't going to be too hard on him after all.

"Well, little Bets, so you're here too, are you?" said the Chief Inspector and patted her head. She caught hold of his hand.

"Inspector Jenks, you won't take Fatty to prison, will you?" she said, in a suddenly choky voice. "He's just been working hard on a mystery, that's all. We all have."

"Cheer up, Bets – I couldn't take him if I tried!" said the Chief. "He's not old enough. Still a kid, you know – bit too big for his boots sometimes, that's all. Well, now, how's everybody? My word, here's a new dog. What's your name, sir?"

"Bingo," said Ern, with such pride in his voice that everyone smiled. "He's *my* dog, sir. My very own.

109

You should see him play with Buster here – they're a pair, they are."

"He's a nice dog, Ern," said the Chief, and patted Bingo, who immediately rolled over on his back in delight. "I gather your uncle doesn't like him. I can't imagine why."

"Nor can I, sir," said Ern. "Sir, you won't let my uncle take him away from me, or anything like that, will you?"

"We'll talk about you and Bingo later," said the Inspector, "and see what can be done. It's Frederick here I'm worried about. This man, Engler, Frederick, certainly has a sound complaint against you. What do you know about him?"

"I know a great deal," said Fatty. "And very surprising it is, sir. The others don't yet know all the things I know – *they'll* be surprised too! I rather think you'll turn your attention to Mr. Engler, sir – and one or two others – when I've finished telling my story!"

Inspector Jenks looked most surprised. He took out his pipe and began to light it, puffing out smoke. Then he sat back comfortably in his chair.

"Tell your story, Fatty," he said, in a much more friendly tone. "I'm ready – no embroidery, mind – just the plain facts – ones that you are absolutely sure of!"

Buster sat up straight, and Bingo sat up straight too. They were going to listen with as much interest as everyone else.

"Well, sir," said Fatty, in a very serious voice. "It all started with the disappearance of a tiny boat in a big picture . . ."

There was dead silence in the shed, as Fatty told the story of the Banshee Mystery.

"It all started with the disappearance of a tiny boat in a big picture in the Picture-Gallery at Banshee Towers," he began.

"A boat in a *picture!*" said the Inspector, astonished.

"Yes, sir. You see, we thought we'd make a few expeditions these holidays, and that was one of them – to Banshee Towers to see the lovely sea-pictures there," went on Fatty.

"It was Ern and I who *really* wanted to go," said Bets.

"So we all went up on our bikes, and paid a shilling to go in. We had a look round – the pictures were grand," said Fatty, "and Ern here stood for ages in front of a very big one . . ."

"Smashing, it was!" said Ern, taking up the story. "And it had a tiny red boat, sir, painted on a wave near the bottom of the picture."

"Well, what about it?" said the Inspector.

"Well, sir, we went again the next day, and I went to look at that picture agan – and the boat was *gone!*" said Ern. "And it wasn't painted out or anything – it just wasn't there."

"Strange," said Inspector Jenks. "You must have made a mistake – looked at another picture perhaps."

"No, sir – Bets here can say the same as me," said Ern, and Bets nodded.

"That was the beginning of the Mystery," said Fatty. "I sort of smelt something fishy from that very moment. I didn't much like the turnstile man, and I certainly didn't like the owner of the pictures, a man called Mr. Engler. And I didn't much like one of the artists there, a Frenchman."

"Oh – there were artists there, were there?" said the Inspector. "Copying the pictures?"

"Yes, sir – but not awfully well, in my opinion," said Fatty. "Except the Frenchman, sir – honestly he was very very good. He wasn't very nice, though – he painted Ern right across the face by slashing at him with his brush. But he was a *real* artist, sir, the others were only art-students from some art-school.

"It said in the catalogue, sir, that the pictures there belonged to a Count Ludwig, of Austria, who had lent them to this Mr. Engler to show in his gallery. Mr. Engler is an Austrian too, I believe. The artists were copying them just for practice, or to sell as copies afterwards. They were most of them awful – I wouldn't have given ten shillings for any of them!" went on Fatty.

"Frederick, you may as well know that we have reason to believe Engler is a crook," said the Chief. "Please tell me straight out if *you* have any reason to believe he is, and if so, WHAT reasons? This is as important for you, as for me."

"All right, sir. I can give you plenty of reasons," said Fatty, briskly. "I'm pretty sure that what he does is to get that French artist to copy the pictures he has had lent to him from various Art galleries all over the place. Then he takes the original picture out of its frame, and rolls it up – and sticks the finished copy in its place – and I must say that François Ortalo makes some wonderful copies!"

"He sells the originals somewhere, for a large sum of

money, of course," said Inspector Jenks. "Just what we suspected – but couldn't prove!"

"Well, you can prove it now, sir," said Fatty. "That French artist made a big mistake when he copied that fine sea-picture that Ern and Bets loved – he forgot to put that tiny boat into the copied picture! That's the *only* difference that Ern and Bets could see in the two pictures!"

"A very, very small omission!" said Inspector Jenks "One that might have gone unnoticed for years – in fact, it might *never* have been spotted. I don't think anyone but sharp-eyed children would notice and remember a tiny boat so clearly! Ern – I congratulate you! You may be the means of catching a very clever and remarkable swindler!"

Ern went as red as a beetroot, tried to say something, and couldn't.

"Of course," went on the Inspector, "we want to know quite a few more things, before we can charge this rogue with stealing. Perhaps you can tell me some of them, Frederick?"

"Well, I don't know, sir," said Fatty. "I *can* tell you a few things, though. The Frenchman's *real* name and address, for instance. I found it in a book when I – er – broke into his bedroom."

Everyone stared at Fatty in surprise. "What's his name – quick, give it to me," said the Chief, opening a notebook.

"His name is François Henri Ortalo, of 91 Rue Carnot, Paris," said Fatty. "He knows all about the famous pictures on the Continent of Europe. I found his name in a book about them."

The Chief gave a little whistle. "Oho – so François Ortalo has turned up here, has he?" he said. "I wouldn't like to say how many different countries want him for

Everyone stared at Fatty in surprise.

swindling people over pictures. Good work, Fatty! Anything else?"

"Well, I know which Art Galleries in America *buy* the original pictures," said Fatty, and gave Inspector Jenks the list he had written down that morning in the office at Banshee Towers.

"Bless my soul!" said the Chief, hardly able to believe his ears. "Am I dreaming? We've been looking everywhere for this information. How in the world do you know this?"

"Well – I just *happened* to see Mr. Engler's office desk," said Fatty, "and I just glanced at a few things, sir."

"I can only hope, Frederick Trotteville, that when you are grown-up, you will join the police-force and not the ranks of the burglars!" said the Inspector. "I suppose you do know that you had no right to go snooping in that fellow's desk, rogue though he is!"

"Well, I wasn't sure, sir," said Fatty, with a twinkle in his eye. "But Ern here was rather shocked, weren't you, Ern?"

"Well, yes, I was," said Ern. "But then I didn't know that Fatty was getting information to pass on to *you*, sir."

"Is there really a Count Ludwig, sir, who lends these pictures to Mr. Engler?" asked Fatty.

"Oh yes," said the Inspector. "And he must be a poor judge of art – because although Engler never sends him back his valuable original pictures, but only dud copies, he has apparently never noticed the difference!"

"Then he won't notice that the tiny little boat is missing when he gets the copy?" said Bets, amazed.

"He certainly won't," said the chief. "You are much smarter than he is, little Bets! And Ern too!"

"Can you charge Mr. Engler – and the artist – and

perhaps the turnstile man – with robbery and swindling?" asked Fatty.

"It's difficult," said the Inspector. "I'd feel safer if I could find out how he gets the original pictures safely out of the Art Galleries he shows them in – such as Banshee Towers, for instance. It isn't easy to smuggle big pictures out of a place you know – or into one, for that matter. It's been really puzzling us. We've watched and watched that fellow – not only here but in other places too – and we've never been able to lay our hands on any pictures being smuggled out or in!"

"Oh, that's easy," said Fatty. "I guessed that early on, sir."

"Fatty! You never told us! *How* did they get the pictures out?" said Larry, astonished.

"Do you remember that there were always lengths of fat lead pipes about – supposed to be for repairs?" said Fatty. "Well, I went and snooped down one – and I saw something tightly rolled up in it – I couldn't imagine then what it was – but now I'm absolutely certain that it was a rolled-up, canvas – a picture off the walls. It wouldn't be missed, for a copy would be immediately slapped into place!"

"FATTY! Remember that ladder this morning – and the cutting sound we heard when we were locked in that room – and the slapping of a brush?" almost shouted Ern, half-leaping from his chair. "That was what they were doing then! They climbed up the ladder to cut the picture out – then they slapped some sort of gluey paste on the empty space – and stretched the copy over it – it stuck almost at once, of course."

"Yes, I remember," said Fatty. "You're quite right, Ern. You've been pretty clever over this."

"Why didn't you tell us all these things?" said Bets.

"Well, I wasn't quite sure how everything fitted,"

116

said Fatty. "You know, it was a bit like a jigsaw. I couldn't see the whole picture, or know what it meant, till I'd found *every* bit of the jigsaw. It wasn't till this morning that I found the last piece – the pipes in the shed! Then at last I knew how they managed to get the pictures out without anyone guessing!"

"You've done remarkably well, Fatty. But I rather fear the men have smelt a rat and gone," said the Chief, shutting his notebook. "Someone must have tipped them that we were on the watch. They went away in a blue van and a car, apparently. The man we had on watch unfortunately wasn't quick enough to take the numbers. So I fear we can't set up road-blocks anywhere, or issue a general warning to the police. We *have* to know the registration numbers of the vehicles."

"Oh those – I nearly forgot," said Fatty. "I saw the numbers this morning. Now – let me see – yes – one was Pair of Rogues, and . . ."

"Pair of Rogues – *that's* not a car-number!" said Larry.

"And the other was Jolly Bad Lot," said Fatty. "Yes – POR 202 and JBL 333, sir. POR for 'Pair of Rogues!' and JBL for 'Jolly Bad Lot'. Easy way to remember those vehicles, sir – the letters described the occupants so well!"

"Well, I won't say what a marvel I think you are, or you *might* get a swelled head," said the Inspector, jotting down the numbers at once. "Do you happen to have memorized the number of *my* car in the same way, Fatty?"

"Yes, sir. Your car number is VGF 888," said Fatty, promptly. "Er – VGF stands for Very Good Fellow, sir."

"Well, I'm glad to hear *that*," said the Inspector, getting up. "Thanks, Fatty, thanks, Ern. We can now pin down those three rogues, and put them somewhere

117

where, I am pretty certain, they will not see many beautiful pictures!"

"What about Mr. Engler's complaint about me, sir?" asked Fatty. "You know – breaking and entering into Banshee Towers. Actually we didn't *break* in, sir – we came up that underground passage."

"Hm: well, in the circumstances, considering that you have given me so much help in this case, Frederick, I shall cross out that complaint in my books," said Inspector Jenks, with a very broad smile indeed. "And you needn't worry about Mr. Goon. I am going straight up to the police station to tell him of the unexpected – and really astonishing – help you have given me this morning. I must say that I think the Five Find-Outers are remarkably good detectives!"

"What about Ern?" asked Bets, anxiously. "Will it be *safe* for him to go back to Mr. Goon's?"

"QUITE safe," said the Inspector. "I shall tell him that his nephew Ern was clever enough to spot what is probably the only clue in existence that could lead to the arrest of a smart rogue like Mr. Engler. Well done indeed, Ern!"

And with that, out went the Inspector, murmuring something to himself. "Let's see now – my car's number is VGF – and Fatty said it stood for Very Good Fellow. Hm – I just wonder what *else* Fatty makes those letters stand for, when I'm *out* of favour. He's certainly worth watching, is Master Frederick Trotteville!"

You never know what Old Fatty is up to!

Mr. Goon was amazed to hear what Inspector Jenks had to say. He simply couldn't believe his ears.

"All those pictures copied, and the originals *sold*! That fellow Engler must have made a fortune. And you say Ern – ERN, my nephew, was the one that spotted the first clue! I'd never have thought it of Ern, never."

"Well, Goon, I shouldn't be surprised if your nephew doesn't make a very fine police-officer in some years' time," said Inspector Jenks, briskly. "It's a pity you scared him so much, and he ran away. He might have been of some use to you."

"Yes, sir. I sort of lost my temper," said Mr. Goon. "I'd like him back, sir. If he's going to be as brainy as you think he is, well, I wouldn't mind teaching him a few things myself, sir, that might be useful to him later on."

"*That's* the way to talk, Goon," said the Chief, getting up, and clapping the policeman on the back. "Youngsters nowadays have some fine stuff in them, you know. As for that boy Frederick Trotteville – well, I pity all the rogues and swindlers and thieves in a few years' time. Once Frederick gets those brains of his to work, they won't have a chance!"

"I think I'll go down to the Trottevilles' house, and have a word with Ern," said Goon, getting up. "His mother's been after me about him, when she heard he wasn't here. Downright angry she was – not with Ern, but with *me*. Just like her sauce!"

"Ah, you just tell her how clever Ern has been – that will smooth her down," said the Inspector. "Well, goodbye, Goon. I'll let you know when we catch those swindlers. You'll have Ern back, of course, and no hard words said on either side. And by the way, what a VERY nice, well-behaved dog he has, hasn't he! Even SITS when he's told. I'm sure you'll enjoy having Bingo back, too, Goon!"

He departed, leaving Mr. Goon feeling rather like a pricked balloon, with the air slowly departing from him. Well, he'd better go down and see those "Find-Outers" as they called themselves. Silly name – but no doubt about it, somehow or other they *did* solve mysteries, and find out extraordinary clues.

"Maybe it's silly of me to go against them," thought Goon, frowning. "Be better if I was more friendly, like, then they'd tell me things. That Ern now – whoever would have thought he had a brain in his head? I can't believe it!"

He set off on his bicycle to ride to Fatty's house, keeping a sharp look-out for dogs. It was a curious thing, but as soon as dogs saw Mr. Goon riding majestically down the road on his old bicycle, they seemed to have but one thought in their doggy minds, and that was to race out into the road at top speed, barking at the top of their voices, and leap at poor Mr. Goon's ankles, as his feet went up and down on the pedals.

Down in the shed no one guessed that Mr. Goon was coming. They were all talking about their adventures in Banshee Towers. "THE most exciting part was where we set off the wailing banshee machinery," said Larry. "My word, that was a clever stunt of Mr. Engler's, wasn't it!"

"I *wish* we had that machinery here," said Fatty. "What a shock everyone would get in the middle of the night!"

"Well, if you particularly *want* to give your neighbours a shock, *you* don't need banshee machinery!"

120

said Pip, giving Fatty a friendly punch. "All you need is your own frightful wail – you're as good as any banshee, Fatty. My word, when you wailed in that Armour Room, the first day we were there, I nearly died of fright!"

"There's only one part of the Mystery we didn't solve," said Larry. "And that was why the banshee apparently chose Thursday for its weekly wail. Why Thursday?"

"Well, apparently there really *wasn't* any mystery about that," said Fatty. "And I needn't have bothered my head over it. Thursday is the turnstile man's half-day off – so he used to set the machinery going to clear everyone away early! Then he'd be able to shut up the place and get off in good time. And I've no doubt that the French artist used to do a bit of packing up then – carefully putting the pictures into those lead pipes, ready for collection."

"Sh! Someone's coming," said Bets. "Oh, Fatty – it's Mr. Goon. Whatever is *he* here for?"

"To complain about me 'harbouring' Ern, I suppose," said Fatty, hurrying to the window at the back of the shed. "Look, I'm not seeing him this morning. I might be a bit rude if he starts saying anything nasty about old Ern. Now you others tell him that Ern's been marvellous, and that even the banshee must have been pretty scared of Ern, and . . ."

"Bang-bang!" That was Mr. Goon knocking at the shed door.

Fatty immediately leapt out of the window with Buster. "If you have any trouble with Goon, don't let it worry you," he said, popping his head through the window. "I'll be listening out here, and I'll come to your help at once."

Larry then opened the door, and there stood Mr. Goon, not looking nearly so fierce as usual. He stepped in, and to everyone's immense astonishment, smiled and nodded.

"Good morning, Mr. Goon," said Bets, politely. The others muttered a greeting too.

"Well, well," said Mr. Goon, in an unexpectedly hearty voice. "Here you all are – oh, except Frederick. I – er – came to congratulate him – and you all – on helping to solve the mystery of Banshee Towers. Ern, I hear that you were quite clever at spotting a very important clue."

Ern blushed bright red at this compliment, and couldn't find a word to say. There was an awkward silence. Bingo broke it by suddenly giving a loud bark, and rushing at Mr. Goon's ankles.

Mr. Goon gave a sickly smile, and tried to push him away. "Bingo," said Ern, suddenly, in a stern voice. "Stop that! SIT!"

And Bingo meekly sat down at once, though he still looked longingly at Mr. Goon's ankles!

"Ha – well-trained dog that," said Mr. Goon, surprised. "Er – I'll be quite pleased to have him back again, Ern. Bring him with you when you come."

There was another awkward and astonished silence. Ern broke it. "Do you really want me to come back, Uncle – and Bingo here, too? He's not a bad dog – just a bit excitable at times, but he's not much more than a pup."

"Oh, he's a fine dog," said Mr. Goon, in a hearty voice. "Very fine. Obedient, too. My word, he must have scared that old banshee! He ha ha!"

Nobody else laughed. They were all still a bit wary of their old enemy.

"Of course, you know," said Goon, "that Banshee business is a bit of a fraud. The sort of thing that Frederick would make a lot of. It's said to wail, I know, but *I've* never heard it whenever I've been near the

Towers! Ho ho – I bet it wouldn't dare to raise its voice if it saw *me* anywhere near!"

"Well, *we* heard it all right," said Bets. "It sounded like – oh, let me see . . . like . . ."

And then, from outside the window, came a little wail. Just a very little one at first. Then it became louder and pitched higher in tone, and soon the little room was full of the most heart-rending, eerie wailing that Goon had ever heard. Bets jumped at first – but she and the others knew at once that it was only old Fatty showing the disbelieving Mr. Goon what a banshee's wail was like!

"Pretend to be scared!" whispered Larry to the others – and at once they clutched one another, and looked so frightened that Mr. Goon felt as if *he* wanted to clutch at somebody too!

Bingo was terrified, and rushed round the room, yelping at the top of his voice, trying to find where the weird noise was coming from. What with the wailing and the barking, and everyone's frightened looks, Mr. Goon was scared out of his life.

"Eeee-oooooooo-oh-oh-oh. eeeeeeeeeeee!" wailed Fatty, enjoying himself thoroughly outside the window. Buster began to yelp as soon as he heard Bingo barking, and when Fatty began another set of wails, Mr. Goon could stand it no longer.

"I'll get help!" he panted. "Someone's in danger!" And out of the door he rushed, and up the garden.

It was most unfortunate that Fatty's mother and the old cook were picking early daffodils in the garden just then. They heard the wailing too, and stood upright at once, listening in fright.

"One of the children had been hurt!" said Mrs. Trotteville. "Oh, what terrible screams and wails! Quick, we must see what's the matter."

So down to the shed they rushed at top speed, just

as Mr. Goon was racing up the path as if wild tigers were after him! They met at a corner, and Mr. Goon was knocked flying by the plump cook. He sat down heavily in a bed of mint, looking most astonished.

"What's happened, what's happened?" cried Mrs. Trotteville. "Has the shed stove fallen over? Has there been an accident?"

But Mr. Goon had no breath to reply. He just went on sitting in the mint, panting loudly, hoping that a banshee wouldn't suddenly appear before him. Poor Mr. Goon!

Mrs. Trotteville and the cook ran to the shed, feeling very anxious indeed. But what in the world was this noise they heard *now*? No wailing – but shrieks of laughter!

"Ha ha ha ha! Oh, I never thought Goon could run like that!"

"Ho ho ho! Good old banshee!"

"Ha ha, ho ho, he he, ho ho . . ." The laughter went on and on, and didn't stop even when Mrs. Trotteville walked into the shed, and gazed round at everyone in indignation.

They had all collapsed into chairs or on the floor. Fatty had climbed back into the room through the window, and was wiping tears from his eyes. He had no breath left to be a wailing banshee any longer! Buster and Bingo had gone completely mad and were barking and tearing round and round the room nonstop.

"FREDERICK! WHAT IS ALL THIS?" demanded Mrs. Trotteville in a very cross voice indeed. She poked at Fatty with a hard forefinger, as he lay collapsed in a chair.

"Oh, Mother, don't. You know I'm ticklish," said Fatty. "Mother, I was only being a banshee. Why are you so cross? It's not against the law to wail like a ban-

124

shee is it?" And off he went again into another roar of laughter.

"I shall fetch your father," said his mother, astounded at Fatty's behaviour. "I really do not know what has come over you all – or Mr. Goon either!"

"Goon – what's he doing that's upset you, Mother!" asked Fatty at once.

"He's sitting down in the very middle of my mint bed, if you want to know," said his mother. "And serve him right too – rushing straight into us like that."

"Sitting down in the *mint* bed, Mother! Oh, this is too good to be true!" said Fatty. "Mother, do you mean to say you pushed him over – oh, Mother, you'll be put into prison if you do things like that. Poor Goon – he'll smell of mint for weeks!"

"Oh, Fatty, please don't make *me* laugh, too," said his mother, feeling a sudden desire to join in the merriment. "I don't know *what* to do with you, Fatty. You're a bad lot. Go and help Mr. Goon out of my mint bed. I'm sure the poor man is still there!"

Yes – there he is, listening in amazement to the laughter coming from Fatty's shed!

"What's happening now? How is it something *always* happens when that fat boy is about?" he grunts. "Pooh, what a smell of mint! One of these days, Master Frederick Trotteville, I'll get the better of you! You see if I don't!"

Well, we'll see next time there's a Mystery to solve, Mr. Goon. But don't be too sure of yourself, will you? You just NEVER know what old Fatty is up to!

THE ENID BLYTON TRUST
FOR CHILDREN

We hope you have enjoyed the adventures of the children in this book. Please think for a moment about those children who are too ill to do the exciting things you and your friends do.

Help them by sending a donation, large or small, to the ENID BLYTON TRUST FOR CHILDREN. The Trust will use all your gifts to help children who are sick or handicapped and need to be made happy and comfortable.

Please send your postal orders or cheques to:

      The Enid Blyton Trust For Children,
      Lee House,
      London Wall,
      London EC2Y 5AS.

Thank you very much for your help.